I0771991

Memories of DAVE'S SAUNA

Written by
Jonathan Leavitt

Thank you Dave and Nancy. Quite a legacy!

Thank you to my parents who introduced me to
Dave's Sauna as a young boy. I never left.
Thank you to Nettie, Sean, and Sara for helping
me bring this book to reality.

Thank you to all the folks who shared their
stories and memories.

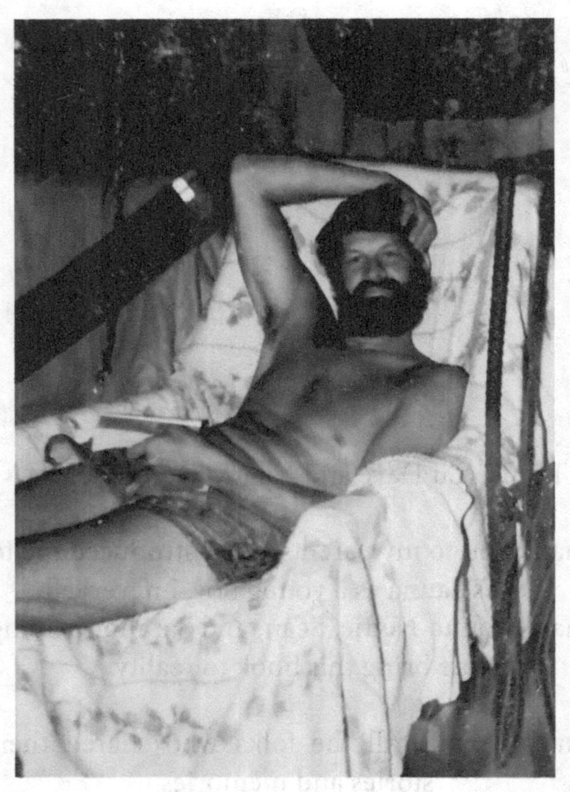

Photo Credits: Nancy Graiver

CONTENTS

While this book is inspired by actual persons and events, certain characters, characterizations, incidents, timelines, locations and dialogue were fictionalized or invented for the purpose of telling a great story!

PROLOGUE

(2008)

Lennie fumbled for a moment with the car radio's knob, before settling on some Tom Petty playing on WCLZ out of Portland. The sun was only half present today, weaving in and out from behind the clouds, its fickle light mirroring his own mixed emotions of sadness and relief. It had been a few months since his father, Dave, had passed, and everyone was still adjusting to a world without him.

After a few miles on one of the busier roads leading toward the outskirts of Norway, he passed a big, old oak tree that always tricked him into thinking he was closer to his dad's place than he really was. Lennie had never understood why his father had chosen to move out to this remote spot a few years ago. Now, he suspected it had been Dave's way of offering Sandy, his girlfriend, something more permanent than the cluttered second-floor apartment he'd built behind the sauna for the two of them.

Still, it was out there, he thought to himself as he finally arrived at Durgin Road, where he sharply turned off the pavement onto what was little more than a bumpy ATV trail. The song on the radio swelled— *"…for the waiting is the hardest part…"*—and Lennie drove past a stretch of low-lying swamp land and overgrown pastures, the kind of forgotten land that hadn't been used in decades.

As he neared the house, the long gravel driveway came into view, and with it, the unfinished structure that had once been his dad's dream. A young collie appeared out of nowhere, running up to greet the car. Lennie regretted not picking up a marrow bone at Hannaford's as an offering.

He slowed, careful not to hit the dog, and parked beside a pile of building materials that had aged less gracefully than the house itself. Turning off the engine, he sat for a moment, staring into the distance. For a brief second, he imagined his father stepping outside to meet him. But it was Sandy's voice—that snapped him out of his daydream.

"Hi, Lennie!" she called, approaching the vehicle with a smile.

"Hey, Sandy," Lennie replied, slowly stepping out of the car, and awkwardly absorbing the hug she offered. Despite their closeness in age, she exuded a maternal comfort that had always been a bit outside his comfort zone. But at this moment, it was exactly what he needed, and he was grateful.

"Come on in," she said, leading him toward the house. The young collie followed, sniffing eagerly at his pant leg, momentarily fooled into thinking Dave might also be emerging from the vehicle.

"You want some coffee?" Sandy asked as they stepped inside, gesturing to the pot sitting on the countertop.

"No, thanks," Dave's son replied, settling onto a stool. "I must've passed a dozen Dunkin' Donuts on my way in from Falmouth. So, I already fell victim to temptation." The collie, who remained still at his feet, looked up at him expectantly, and Lennie reached down to give him a few pats. "Okay, boy. Go lie down now." The pup trotted under the kitchen table where he made himself comfortable.

"Is this the stuff you mentioned?" Lennie asked, pointing to a couple of milk crates sitting on the kitchen table, stacked with what looked like a collection of paperback books.

"Yup. That's everything," Sandy said. "Unless you want his collection of shorts!" she added, and they shared a laugh, as they both realized how difficult it was to imagine Dave wearing anything but his usual uniform—cut-off blue jean shorts and work boots.

His son grinned sheepishly. "I don't think I could pull off the look quite like Dad did. Maybe we can find a museum putting together an exhibit on the mating rituals of 1970s back-to-the-land Jewish hippies, and donate them?" he chuckled, walking over to the crates and beginning to sift through the contents.

Sandy smiled knowingly as she poured herself a cup of coffee. "Sure," she laughed nervously, "We can throw in his EZ chair, a few unwashed t-shirts, and the stick of unused deodorant that sat on the bathroom shelf for as long as I knew him!"

Lennie paused and smiled. "It's toasty in here," he remarked, feeling the warmth of the kitchen. "I'm guessing you're free to turn up the thermostat now?"

Sandy raised an eyebrow, acknowledging the truth in his words. "Yeah," she said, her voice softening a little. "It was kind of like a going-away present."

Dave's oldest son nodded, and for a moment, there was a quiet stillness. He picked up one of the photo albums, and his eyes began flicking over the pages. But the memories were too much, too soon, and he wasn't ready. He sighed deeply, set the album back in the crate, and gently pushed it aside.

For the next fifteen minutes, they made small talk, before the conversation began to slowly wind down. Finally, after another awkward pause, Lennie stood up. "I think I'll grab these and head out," he said, moving toward her boxes and loading them in his arms before she could react.

Sandy tried masking ger disappointment. She had been hoping for some extended time to share her grief with someone in the family. With Dave gone, the connection between her and his kids was already feeling fragile.

"Oh, okay," she said, her voice laced with a hint of hurt. "Do you need help loading them in your car? They're heavier than they look."

"No, I got it," Lennie replied, his voice gentle but final. "But thanks."

"Here — Let me at least get the door for you," she said, setting her coffee down and walking ahead of him.

Once the crates were loaded in the car, Dave's son turned to the pup one last time and gave him a final scratch behind the ears. He turned back to Sandy. "I think Dad would be glad we're taking all this stuff. That we can hold onto some of the memories."

"Agreed," she said, stepping back from the vehicle. "Take care, Lennie."

"You too, Sandy," Lennie let his hand linger on the door handle before starting the engine. As the radio hummed to life, he made a quick three-point turn and watched his father's house slowly fade from view in the rearview mirror.

I'M JUST A JEWISH REFUGEE

**"I'm Just a Jewish Refugee
Running from US savagery
Now my best friends are some trees
Look Ma what's become of me"**

(1976)

The late morning sun was shining brightly, and the last stubborn remnants of winter's harsh grip had finally loosened their hold on the trees. It was spring in western Maine, with all sorts of life emerging from hibernation, and the earth itself exhaling a deep, rejuvenating breath. Perennials began to stretch from the ground, their colors returning to the landscape like a quiet promise.

As Dave cruised through the quiet, winding streets of the old boarding town of Paris, the window of his 1972 Vega cracked open just enough to let in the crisp, earthy scent of the thawing soil. The smell was a balm for his soul—offering both forgiveness for the months of cold and the intoxicating possibility of something new.

But the fleeting moment of peace didn't last long.

No sooner had Dave crossed the train tracks that divided the town in two, than a sharp, unmistakable stench hit him—an odor that quickly brought him back to reality. It was the unmistakable smell of the local tannery, thick and sour, reminding him of the town's less appealing side. It was a scent that many old timers had long grown accustomed to. But for Dave, it felt like a rude awakening and the pleasant promise of spring quickly faded and his thoughts, once light and open, narrowed once more.

The nagging question that had been circling in his mind for

days now resurfaced: *What's next?* It was a question that had been haunting him for months, and no matter how many times he tried to push it aside, it kept creeping back in, like an unwelcome guest.

By now it had been a couple of years since his first wife, Rachel, had packed up and returned to Boston with their two-year-old son, Lennie, after finding Dave in bed with two of her best friends. Since then, he'd bided his time in their makeshift cabin in Norway, passing the days smoking the weed he'd grown, playing softball with the hillbilly neighbors, and taking long, aimless walks in the woods.

And for a while, it felt like enough. Making money wasn't urgent, and life seemed manageable without too much of it around. But now, with his thirtieth birthday just around the corner, realities were starting to creep in—child support obligations, living expenses, and the growing weight of his parents' nagging about finding some direction. They were right, of course. But Dave still had no clue where he fit in.

Long-haired folk like him didn't have many options, and for a long-haired Jewish guy with little patience for authority, the choices were even slimmer. He thought about his last attempt at holding down a job. Rachel's father, worried about Dave's lack of motivation, had landed him a gig at Purity Supreme, a big supermarket in Massachusetts. Dave had given it a try, riding his Kawasaki 185 into the city each week, unloading trucks for long hours, then rushing back to Maine for the weekend to be with his wife. But the honeymoon phase didn't last.

Dave couldn't stand his boss, Mr. Dyer. Every correction, every directive from him, felt like a personal attack. After about a month, he had had enough. One grueling day of unloading heavy boxes, Dave threw up his hands and told his supervisor to *go to hell.* Working for a boss was unlikely to be part of the answer.

There were other ideas—other possibilities he had considered. Like many of the young hippies who'd come to western Maine, he had dabbled in growing pot. At first, it was just enough for his own head stash. But over the years it had grown into a small side business and according to his friends, his weed was better than most of the other locally grown, so there was real potential.

The problem was, Dave didn't have the temperament for farming. It wasn't the work or the weather. It was the waiting. Growing weed meant waiting more than half the year for a return on your crop. Along the way there were dozens of potential pitfalls that included losing it all overnight to mold, having it stolen by local teenagers, or getting popped by law enforcement. As much as he enjoyed gardening, it just didn't hold the same thrill when there was so much on the line.

He'd also thought about carpentry. He'd learned the basics when he and Rachel had built their house, and had enjoyed the work and the fact that it didn't require taking orders from anyone.

But the market in Maine was flooded with people like him— self-taught carpenters who could fix a roof or build a shed, but without the credentials or drive to land steady contractor work. To really make it as a carpenter, he'd have to become a Master Carpenter and that meant years of apprenticeship. It also meant being bossed around by demanding customers from out of state who had no idea what they were talking about. It wasn't a good fit.

Dave's mind continued to wander as he drove west on Route 26 toward Paris Hill, the home of the local aristocracy—whom Dave liked to call the *muckity mucks*. Once upon a time, Paris Hill had been home to Hannibal Hamlin, Abraham Lincoln's first vice president. But these days, its only claim to fame was the spectacular view of Mount Washington, an old stone jail, and the kind of smug entitlement that ran through its residents' bloodlines, like a disease.

Dave couldn't stand most of the people living up there. It wasn't that he had a problem with wealth—he respected hard-earned money. But the old-money arrogance that ran through Paris Hill rubbed him the wrong way. The way they looked down on anyone without a storied family history reminded him too much of the elitism he'd grown up with in the suburbs of Boston.

Lost in thought, Dave nearly missed the turn onto Paris Hill Road. At the last second, he jerked the wheel, crossing the narrow bridge over the Little Androscoggin River. The road ahead rose sharply, and he punched the gas. As he passed a small, nondescript building on the left, something caught his eye—a *For Sale* sign in the window. Above the door, another sign read: *Dick's Sauna*. Curious, Dave downshifted and turned into the parking lot. He pulled the Vega to a stop and stepped out, stretching his legs before surveying the place.

The building was nothing special—a single-story structure sitting low on a slab foundation, its faded wood siding peeling in places. The gravel parking lot, large enough to accommodate maybe a dozen cars, was scattered with patches of overgrown weeds, suggesting it hadn't seen much traffic recently. Trees lined the right side of the property, their leaves just beginning to bud, and a small driveway snaked up the hill toward the neighbor's house.

The picture windows, clouded with dust, caught the late afternoon light, casting a soft, golden glow that filtered through the grime. Dave could make out the faint flicker of a woodstove in the corner, its warmth almost visible, casting a welcoming light across the otherwise dim room. Even from the outside, the place felt inviting—calm, almost womb-like, and a quiet refuge from the outside world.

He pushed open the front door, and a musty scent hit him, mingling with the faint smell of wood smoke. Inside was a small, sparsely furnished lounge area that reminded him of the sugar shack his neighbor had, with mismatched chairs and weathered wood floors. He walked across the room and peered down a narrow corridor with doors lining each side of the hall. In front of every other door was small stack of kindling neatly placed outside.

"Can I help you?" A voice from inside of the rooms startled him, pulling him out of his thoughts.

Dave didn't waste any time. "How much?"

————

A few days later, Dave returned to Dick Kenny's sauna to discuss the details.

Dick had opened the sauna a few years ago, facing competition from a similar one just up the hill and another over in Oxford. At first, it mainly attracted second- and third-generation Finnish immigrants, still holding on to old-world traditions. Over time, Dick learned the story of the original Finnish settlers in Oxford County, beginning with Jakobi Mikkonen, who had emigrated from Finland in 1898. Mikkonen ended up in Paris, Maine, after being tossed off a freight train passing through. He picked up an axe and started chopping wood, eventually settling in West Paris. The Finns who soon followed him to the area brought their traditions with them, including the sauna.

The sauna was more than just a way to get warm in the brutal winters. For the Finns, it was a place of health and healing—relieving muscle pain, improving circulation, clearing the airways. But it was also a community space where people came together, sweat mingling with conversation and camaraderie. It was where friendships were solidified, worries were shared, and generations were united.

Over the past decade, the sauna had attracted a new wave of customers — hippies who had fled the cities looking for space to live and breathe. They'd embraced the sauna for the same reasons the Finns had: an escape from the grind of modern life, and a place to relax, unwind, and connect.

Despite all this, Dick was barely scraping by and was ready to get out. His soon-to-be wife had no faith in the sauna's potential, and he knew it wasn't going to get any easier. He was going to have to either unload the sauna, or his fiancée. After a few weeks of indecision, the *For Sale* sign had gone up. By the time Dave returned a week later, Dick was more than willing to negotiate. After a few hours, a deal was struck and the selling price was set for $35,000, financed over several years.

As he drove back to his cabin in North Norway, Dave felt good about his investment. After all, he already had a side business selling dime bags, and the sauna could only help to bring in more customers for his side hustle. And on a more urgent level, it would give him an excuse to be around scantily clad women on a nightly basis, something he was eager to have back in his life.

———

A month later, the sign outside read *Dave's Sauna*. Now all that was left was for him to *learn how to start a fire* as Dick would joke for years.

CHAPTER 2
ASK ME WHY, I'LL SAY, "WHY NOT?"

*"Growing up in the hills meant a couple of things
You never knew what tomorrow would bring
And if you didn't get out you had to make your peace
With any kind of future mostly out of your reach
So, when anyone asks me why, I say why not?"*

(1977)

Being a bachelor did have its perks—freedom, spontaneity, and even the occasional late-night adventure. But there were certain elements of domestic life that Dave found himself longing for, things he hoped he might eventually have once again. And he was reminded of this daily, most glaringly during breakfast, lunch, and dinner.

Not being one to follow the rules, even with a cookbook, Dave's meals were often more chaotic than culinary triumphs. Usually resulting in a plate of something inedible or a kitchen full of dishes that were more effort than they were worth. So, despite his aversion to spending money on things he could technically do himself, his stomach—more than his stubbornness—would often win, convincing him to bite the bullet and go out to eat.

Whenever that happened, he would find himself at the Country Way Restaurant, situated a mile away in what passed for a downtown in Paris, Maine. It was a seat-yourself kind of establishment with a friendly and bustling staff serving breakfast all day. Very often, his buddy Saul, who he jokingly referred to as the only other Jewish hippy in Oxford Hills, would join him.

Saul was also from away, and he had inherited a small parcel of land in West Paris from a grandfather barely known to him during his lifetime. Currently he was also doing his best carving out a living from some rudimentary carpentry skills and the annual harvest of a dozen or so marijuana plants he had scattered on his property.

But his real passion was the organic vegetable garden and fruit trees now growing in his backyard. Through a significant amount of reading over the long Maine winters, and the sometimes-painful trial and error of spring and summer, Saul was almost making it work. There was no income yet, but after only a few years in, he was managing to grow most of his own food, and his goal of self-sufficiency was finally becoming plausible.

———

"Can I get you boys anything to drink?" Nancy asked, with a warm and friendly voice, as she approached their table. She was a tall, lanky waitress with blonde hair pulled into a loose ponytail, her uniform slightly askew but somehow adding to her charm. Dave had been eyeing her for months, always making sure to sit in her section, hoping for a chance to strike up a conversation.

He started with the usual small talk, and her smile—always genuine and inviting—gave him enough encouragement to keep trying, and leading him to believe, even if just for a moment, that his efforts weren't entirely unnoticed.

Dave guessed that Nancy was in her early twenties, and by the relaxed, almost effortless way she carried herself, it was clear she was a local. She had the hands of a do-it-yourself kind of girl—clean but calloused in all the right places. Dave figured she could probably change a flat tire without breaking a sweat, a skill he knew was always a big turn-on for first-generation Mainers. As he watched her move around the diner, he decided that tonight—finally, after months of casual glances and small talk—he was ready to make a move and attempt some kind of seduction over the course of his meal.

"I'll have a glass of orange juice and the country fried steak…," said Saul, in a gentle voice, "…with mashed potatoes and a side of broccoli," he finished, setting down his menu with a satisfied nod, as if he'd made the decision days ago.

"And for you?" asked Nancy, now turning to Dave, who had been patiently waiting for her to catch his eyes.

"Surprise me!" Dave said, leaning back in his chair, his grin widening as he watched her. His voice was playful, but there was something behind the words—something that made Nancy pause.

The waitress blushed, with a hint of nervousness creeping into her smile. "I'm not very good at surprises," she said, her voice a little softer. "Do you want your usual?" Her familiarity with his dining history sent a strange flutter through Dave. She was paying attention.

"Nope!" said Dave, his voice more forceful now. "I want whatever you would make for your boyfriend. What does he like to eat?"

Nancy froze for a moment, caught off balance. She didn't have a boyfriend. Not anymore. And she hadn't expected Dave's question to land so sharply. Her mind briefly wandered to the last time she had agreed to a date with one of her Country Way regulars. The memory was enough to temper any excitement.

It had started innocently enough, with her date arriving to pick her up in a truck that proudly rattled every time it hit a bump. There was a gun rack bolted just above the back window and a cooler full of PBR sat in the truck bed. After a brief detour to help a buddy who was in the middle of changing out a transmission, they ended up at the Oxford Plains Speedway.

Her memory grew fuzzier after that, but she was almost certain that after all the excitement that loud engines and fried food could offer, the evening had wrapped up with unprotected sex on some skidder trail in Norway.

Like more than a few young romances, passion and hormones had overridden common sense, and the relationship had ended in a rushed marriage lasting less than a year.

Nancy felt her stomach tighten, and she shook off the memory, and returned to the present where Dave was still waiting for an answer.

For now, she thought it best to evade his question. "Okay then, I'll do my best to surprise you tonight." She stuffed her check pad into her side pocket, smiled, and turned away.

"What was that all about?" Saul asked, raising an eyebrow as he gestured toward Nancy's retreating figure.

"What?" Dave asked, still grinning, a little more to himself now than anyone else.

"Let's hope she doesn't bring you any pork chops!" Saul snickered, nudging him playfully.

"Yup…" Dave said, a wry grin creeping onto his face. "…I wouldn't want to feel the full force of the good old Lord's wrath like you did!" he added, referencing the recent lightning strike that had obliterated the wind turbine Saul had painstakingly built from wood, scrap metal, and old auto parts.

The comment sparked a heated debate over the practicality of wind power. Saul, ever the optimist, was predictably eager to rebuild the rig. Dave, on the other hand, had been arguing for months that the technology just wasn't practical yet—regardless of what his buddy had read in *Mother Earth News*.

"Yeah, see you gotta cut your losses and, well… *stop tilting at windmills*," Dave chuckled.

As the conversation waned, so did Dave's focus. Instead, he decided that he would be much better off following Nancy's movement from across the room and watching her hips sway from table to table.

"Dave!" said Saul, giving his friend a knowing look and snapping his fingers. "Are you even listening?"

"To be honest? Not really," said Dave dryly.

Before Saul could react, a short, round, and busty waitress with red hair and apple cheeks arrived at their table with a tall glass of orange juice and a cold ice water. "Alrighty," she chirped cheerfully. "Busy night tonight boys, hope you don't mind me helping with your table. Now, who had the orange juice?"

Saul nodded and gestured with a hand. The waitress placed his beverage down in front of him. "I take it the ice water must belong to this handsome fella?" she said smiling at Dave.

"Thanks Betsy," he replied.

"Why of course! Anything for my favorite sauna guy," the waitress pronounced joyfully. "I'm hoping to get over there sometime this weekend with the gals… providing I can find a sitter for the kids," she gave Dave a wink.

"By gals, I hope you mean your waitress friend over there!" Dave said slyly nodding in Nancy's direction.

"Now wouldn't that be a hoot!" declared Betsy. "But truthfully, I was actually thinking about asking her to babysit."

"Betsy! Order up!" called a voice from the back kitchen.

"Back to the grind boys. But don't you worry, one of us should be out here with your dinner soon!" She spun around and headed back to the kitchen.

By now, Saul had given up on sharing any sort of meaningful conversation with his friend and was simply hiding behind the pages of the *Advertiser Democrat*, carefully reading the obituaries.

To kill time Dave, flipped over the place mat in front of him, pulled out a pen from his pocket and began to make a list of things he needed to do on the following day…*Chop more firewood… Pick up a load of kindling from over in Greenwood…Fill kindling buckets…Jimmy-rig the door in Sauna 6…Pick up weed from you know who…*

His concentration was broken when he heard Nancy's voice behind him, causing a welcoming blood rush to the more troublesome part of Dave's anatomy. "Here you are boys!" said Nancy balancing two hot plates in her hands.

Dave flipped his paper placemat back over and she placed his dinner on top.

"Sorry for the wait," Nancy sighed apologetically.

"I'm sure it will be worth it," Dave reassured her.

"Thank you!" said Saul who was feeling like a third wheel and more than ready to get started on the meal.

"Careful, it's hot!" Nancy warned, her voice light but insistent as she set the steaming dish down in front of Saul. She didn't look at him—her eyes flicking quickly to Dave instead as she tucked a stray lock of her long blonde hair behind her ear. "I hope you like chicken potpie," she added, her smile just a touch too bright.

"This looks fantastic!" Dave exclaimed, offering her a grin that was almost too wide. "It's like you read my mind!"

It wasn't true, of course. He was more of a meat-and-potatoes guy than anything else. But if he had any hope of getting closer to her, a little flattery—however exaggerated—was a small price to pay.

Across the table, Saul had had enough. His fork moved lazily around the mound of mashed potatoes, stirring them into a sad, sloppy heap. "Yeah, read your mind, huh?" he grumbled, his voice tinged with obvious sarcasm.

Dave didn't engage and instead turned back to Nancy. "Well," he continued, "I'm sure it's going to taste as good as it looks." He leaned back slightly in his chair, eyes meeting hers for just a moment longer than necessary, before glancing down at the dish in front of him.

Saul couldn't take it any longer. "I gotta go to the little boy's room," he announced before putting his fork down and climbing out from the booth, silently swearing that he'd be eating dinner solo the next time his friend invited him out.

Nancy ignored Saul's obvious frustration and let out a little laugh. This was all Dave needed. *It's now or never,* he thought, sensing an opening. He leaned in, lowering his voice to what he imagined was just above a whisper. "Speaking of reading minds," he began, glancing over at the waitress with a playful grin. "Got any plans for the weekend? I know Betsy's on the hunt for a babysitter again, but if you're in the mood for something a bit more... adult, I've got a few ideas."

Despite his best intentions, the volume of his voice carried well beyond the booth they shared, and customers at neighboring tables went silent as they waited for an answer from Nancy.

The audacity of this guy! To put it all out there in public like that... she thought as Dave's question was having an odd effect—making her feel both exposed and, intrigued. The silence between them stretched on uncomfortably until, finally, he broke it again.

"What do you say?" pried Dave. "Do you want to do something this weekend?"

With the ball now squarely in her court, Nancy paused, weighing the offer. Life in Oxford Hills wasn't particularly challenging for her, but breaking free from the monotony seemed unlikely without a little push. And Dave was indeed different then the men she was used to dating and certainly not the type to consider bagging a sixteen-point buck to be the highlight of their life. He was also quite the physical specimen with the cutoff jean shorts he always wore, leaving very little to the imagination.

She leaned forward across the table, closing the distance between them, and in a voice far more measured than his, simply replied, "Why not?"

CHAPTER 3

COME CLEAN UP YOUR ACT

"Bring your own towels it'll save you a buck
I got a room open, so I guess you're in luck
I'll even wipe it down, so you don't get stuck
*Heard the neighbor complaining still don't give a *%$#@#"*

(1978)

Where the hell did I put it? Dave thought to himself, his frustration growing with each passing second. He tossed aside a jumble of items in the junk drawer—old receipts, stray paper clips, and random knick-knacks that had taken up residence. A rubber band snapped to the floor along with a few coins, rolling away as if mocking his disorganization. "Someone really needs to clean out this fucking drawer," he grumbled, kneeling to scoop up the coins, and shoving them into his pocket without thinking.

He moved over to his EZ chair, and picked up a large, empty envelope from the side table, shaking it slightly hoping the missing contents might magically appear. It was the third time trying this, in as many minutes, and each time the envelope remained stubbornly empty. An uneasiness started taking root in his stomach.

Since Nancy had moved in just over a year ago, his organizational skills—or lack thereof—had gone to hell. True, her hard work and warm presence had sparked a renewed sense of purpose in him: a new ambition for life, work, and family. It had even made his ex-wife Rachel comfortable enough to send their son for weekends and summer visits, something Dave had always looked forward to.

But at the moment, none of that mattered. He now assumed that her tidying up around the sauna—something he used to never care about—was probably behind the disappearance of the cash and it was causing him to re-evaluate his recent invitation for her to come live their full time.

Frustrated, Dave pushed his thoughts aside and refocused on the task at hand—getting the saunas ready for use. Thankfully, he'd managed to get the stoves fired up earlier in the afternoon, a small victory in the midst of his mounting irritation. But there were still buckets to fill and wood to stack, promising him a welcome distraction from the gnawing sense of worry that was settling in.

But he couldn't let go of the missing money, and he found himself pacing the narrow hall between sauna rooms, trying to remember where he had last handled it. He peaked his head into the laundry room where an old mattress was leaning against the wall. It had previously belonged to Dave's grandfather, and he and Nancy would pull it out for sleeping. Dave tilted the mattress with a frustrated grunt, so he could get a look behind it. But there was only dust and dirty towels as far as his eyes could see, and he released the mattress from his grip.

His search was cut short when the bell above the front door jingled and a familiar voice shouted, "Hello?".

"I'm back here, Tim!" Dave called from the laundry room. A few seconds later, a wiry guy with thinning brown hair, appeared in the doorway of the room.

"Haven't seen you in a while," Dave remarked while mentally crossing the laundry room off his list of potential hiding spots.

Tim's lean, muscular frame was the result of a decade spent in the Navy. Like Dave, he'd been through a failed marriage and currently considered himself married to his boat—life was simpler that way.

"Just got back from a hellish trip across the Atlantic!" Tim said. "But more about that later. What exactly are you doing? You look a little flustered," he curiously noted.

"Just trying to figure out where the hell my money went. I can't find ten grand I had around here somewhere," Dave admitted.

It wasn't the kind of thing he would share with just anyone, but Tim was a trusted friend—and the only other person who had the combination to the sauna's safe. Like Dave, Tim was originally from Massachusetts, but more importantly, they shared a commitment to never allowing a bad law to get in the way of a good entrepreneurial opportunity.

"Where was the last place you had it?" Tim sounded unfazed, as if he already knew the outcome of his friend's dilemma.

Dave gave him a look. "Really?

"Okay, man, just trying to be helpful," Tim said, raising his hands in mock surrender. "Look, Dave, I'm a smuggler, not a detective!"

Tim had earned that title soon after he joined the Navy at seventeen and began serving on a submarine. He and his crew would sneak cases of Cuban rum into King's Bay, Georgia, a profitable operation that was a nice perk on top of his government paycheck. After civilian life had bored him for a decade, he had returned to his roots as the excitement and the payoff werethe perfect storm for him.

"You want a sauna?" Dave asked, shifting gears.

"Uh… yeah, I guess a sauna would be nice," Tim replied.

He heard the jingle of the front door. "Here we go!" he muttered, reluctantly leaving his search for the cash behind.

Both men walked back into the main room, where Ben and Kelly, a biker couple who had been regulars for years, were waiting. Since opening the sauna, Dave had become good friends with at least a dozen members of the local MC thanks mostly to the couple's steady visits and introductions.

"Dave!" Ben called. He was a towering figure with a sun-kissed, heavily tattooed arm that he extended. Dave shook his hand and felt grateful to be on good terms.

"Hi, Dave!" Kelly chirped, kissing him on the cheek. Her curly blonde hair bounced as she moved, and she smelled of perfume and cigarettes.

"Just the two of you today?" Dave asked. He was surprised there wasn't a third person in tow, which was generally their norm.

"Yup…" Ben said, glancing over at Tim. "…unless he wants to join us?"

Kelly giggled, and Tim blushed slightly, embarrassed by the suggestion. "Thanks for the offer, but I'm good," he said, leaning against the bar.

"Your loss," Kelly teased, giving him a wink. "It's not often my husband invites another man into our sauna."

That was true, Dave thought. As far as he could recall, it had always been a woman who had accompanied them on their visits, although rarely the same one.

"Got any hot ones ready to go? And don't be stingy with the wood, Dave—I know where you sleep!" Ben joked, pointing to the floor beneath them with a laugh.

"Hey now!" Dave shot back defensively. "It's temporary. I told Nancy we're moving upstairs once the work is done!" He was feeling a bit defensive about the housing situation after recent events.

He didn't offer any additional details to the bikers. But a few months earlier, Dave had decided to raise the roof on the one-story building and add a couple rooms upstairs to live in and rent out. Unfortunately, he had mistakenly cut one of the trusses at which point he had decided that it would be best to hire someone with more experience. The near disaster only confirmed his decision a few years back that being a carpenter wasn't the smartest path for his new life in Maine.

"Let's get you guys into sauna five," Dave said, motioning toward the door. "I know it's your favorite and I'll wipe the dust off the window so people can get a good look!" he semi-joked.

Turning back to Tim, he said "You get room thirteen. Grab a bucket of wood on your way in."

Tim laughed. The price of true friendship with Dave meant having to get your own sauna hot.

———

After their sauna session, Ben and Kelly returned to the main room, their skin flushed and red from the heat. Dave wasn't exactly sure what went on behind the sauna door, but as he watched the couple sip on his infamous, piss-warm, dirt-cheap beers at the bar, he chuckled to himself, briefly imagining the chaos. Thirty minutes later, the couple finished their drinks, exchanged their goodbyes, and slipped out into the cool evening air.

As Dave was clearing their empty cans, he saw that Kelly had left her biker jacket draped over the back of the bar stool. *That's not going to go over well at the homestead*, he thought. He grabbed a bowl of grapes from the fridge and glanced over at the clock. He was expecting Nancy would be back soon, and he was really hoping that she might bring something home for dinner—a sandwich, maybe, or at least something that didn't taste like cardboard.

Before hunger could fully settle in, Tim appeared in the doorway, dressed and freshly showered, his wet hair still dripping and a used towel carelessly slung over his shoulder.

"How was it?" Dave offered him his usual line.

"Good... and I really needed a shower," Tim replied, looking a little uncomfortable. "There wasn't much hot water down in my sauna, though. But you already knew that didn't you?"

Dave ignored the question. "So, what brings you here? It's not the weekend."

Tim glanced around, double checking that the room was empty. "I've got something big," he said, stretching out the last word for emphasis before pausing. "I thought maybe we could help each other out."

Dave's curiosity was piqued, and he took a seat at the bar, pushing the bowl of grapes in his friend's direction.

Tim declined the offer and instead he picked up a loose pen from the countertop and started rolling it between his thumb and fingers.

"I sailed back into Portsmouth this weekend, but my usual connection wasn't there. Just vanished... I don't know if he got picked up by the cops or what. But now I'm stuck with a boatload of Moroccan hash and a crew of three ex-felons who want to get paid." He took a moment to catch his breath before continuing.

"There aren't a lot of people I trust in this world. But I trust you. And your place—this setup—it's perfect. No one would suspect a thing." Tim looked at him, hopeful. "You want to help me move it?"

There was a hint of desperation in his voice, making it clear just how urgent the situation was.

But Dave wasn't sure he could help, considering that most of his business was on a much smaller scale. "Shit!" he muttered. "I sell dime bags. How the hell am I supposed to move all that hash?"

Tim leaned in, lowering his voice to a whisper. "Come on, Dave. Think about all the people who come through here! With what you've got going on, there's no one in Maine who's got a better setup for something like this."

Dave stayed silent for a moment, considering. His gut told him his buddy was right, but the anxiety radiating off his friend was significant. This would be a hell of risk, especially with that much product. He would need to cultivate a significant amount of now out-of-state customers to guarantee success and that meant a lot of exposure.

As he continued to mull Tim's offer, his eyes wandered and landed on Kelly's leather jacket draped across the bar stool. *The bikers!* he thought. Sure, as hell, they'd buy it. Despite their rough exterior, he knew the bikers ran a tight ship. And if they didn't have the cash on hand, their brothers up in Montreal most certainly would.

Trusting his gut had served him well in the past, and in that moment, Dave decided there was no reason to stop now. "Ok. I'm in."

"Good…Oh, and I found this in the changing room." Tim casually set a thick stack of bills down on the bar. "Look familiar?"

———

A few days later, as the sun was setting, a U-Haul truck pulled up in front of Dave's parents' house in Sharon, Massachusetts, carrying two anxious men and a large quantity of Moroccan hash hidden in moving boxes. After a quick hello to let his folks know that of his arrival, Dave backed the truck up to the garage doors. With his folks fully absorbed watching the *Love Boat*, he and Tim got busy unloading the boxes that they had agreed to store for a few months.

Dave had decided his folk's garage would be a much safer storage spot for drugs than the sauna. After all, law enforcement was unlikely to be sniffing around a place like this, with most local criminal activity confined to high-stakes contracts, lawyers, and banks.

His parents weren't exactly American nobility, but they had climbed high enough on the ladder to be comfortable. Dave's father, Frankie, was a retired chemical engineer, while his mother, Queenie, imagined herself as a proper upper-class British lady. Recently, she'd even gone so far as to offer Nancy ten thousand dollars to call off the wedding to her son. The pedigree wasn't a good fit, she had explained to her husband after he questioned her actions.

After filling up the garage with plastic bins, Dave and Tim threw a tarp over the containers and sat in silence. A few minutes later they joined Dave's parents in the kitchen and caught up over a shared dinner of baked chicken, asparagus, and roasted potatoes.

After about an hour of small talk, the men began preparing for the trip back to Maine. Before he could escape, Queenie pulled her son aside with a subtle, knowing smile. "You're really sure about Nancy, aren't you?"

Dave blinked, momentarily taken off guard by the question. "What do you mean, Mom?"

She lowered her voice, her eyes narrowing thoughtfully. "I just wonder if you're sure she's the right choice for you. I know you're smitten, but...it's a big decision."

Dave was unsure how to respond. "She's... good for me," he finally said, trying to keep his voice steady. "She pushes me to be better. I need that."

Queenie studied him for a long moment before nodding, her expression softening. "Well, just remember, Dave, that love is a lot like a house. It's only as strong as the foundation it's built on."

Dave felt the weight of her words but nodded. "I know, Mom. I'll make sure it's solid."

She gave him a quick, warm hug.

"I'll see you guys soon," Dave promised his parents. "I'll have more room up north soon. I'm just in the middle of some construction at the sauna and I didn't want any of this stuff to get damaged during the transition."

"Make it a weekend trip next time – and bring my grandson along!" Queenie, insisted. After she closed the door, she went and locked the garage. She wasn't certain what was in the boxes, but knowing her son, it was best that she simply ignored that kind of nagging question.

Anyways, if it meant seeing her son more, what did it really matter?

CHAPTER 4

I GOT BEER BEHIND THE COUNTER

"I got beer behind the counter – but it's not very cold
I got beer behind the counter – and that's illegal I'm told
I got beer behind the counter – bought cheap out of state
I guess one man's dreams is another man's fate"

(1979)

Dave huffed along with the rhythm of his ax, each swing steady and determined, before pausing to wipe the sweat from his brow. Taking a moment to appreciate his own hard work, he turned to admire the large pile of freshly split wood, and inhaled a long, deep breath, letting the earthy, rich scent fill his lungs.

"Lennie —" called Dave, aiming in the direction of the wetland trees that buffered the river behind the sauna. "…that's good for today," he stated. But his young son, in his button-down overalls and mud-covered boots, was too intent on his quest of filling a kindling bucket with sticks.

"Lennie!" shouted Dave again, but this time just a little bit louder. His son looked up from his work. "That's good for now!" reaffirmed his dad. "Nancy left us sandwiches inside and then we gotta get on the road." The young boy tossed one last stick into the five-gallon bucket and scampered up from the wetlands like an excited golden retriever.

A few minutes later, they stood in the sauna parking lot. "Where are we going?" Lennie asked, wiping the remnants of peanut butter and jelly from his face.

Dave finished loading up a tarp into the back of the sauna truck before responding. "Just hop in. We're going to New Hampshire on a beer run!" There was a hint of conspiracy in his tone.

"A beer run?" his son replied with a confused look on his face. In his mind he imagined cans of beer with long cartoon legs and arms engaged in a race of some kind. "What are they running from?"

Dave laughed. "They are running from the law Lennie. Cuz that's what you gotta do sometimes!"

He was happy to see his boy so excited and glad that he had waited for him to return from his mother's house in Massachusetts before making the trip across the border. It was a trip he made every few weeks to buy cases of beer in the neighboring state, where there was no sales tax. He would then turn around and illegally resell it at the sauna, which had no liquor license. Dave knew that shady business like this was best done with a child along for the ride and this trip certainly qualified.

The two of them climbed into the cab of the truck. "Hey Lennie, ever drive before?" His son's eyes lit up with his father's question. This was something his mother would never let him do. "Climb up and I'll teach you!" Dave offered enthusiastically.

Without hesitation, the boy jumped onto his dad's lap, and minutes later they pulled out of the sauna parking lot. For a short stretch, oncoming vehicles were met with the bewildering sight of two heads behind the wheel of a vehicle, before Dave regained control and Lennie moved back to the passenger seat, where he slumped to his side and gazed out the window.

As the truck rumbled through the western Maine foothills, the towering presence of the White Mountains began looming on the horizon, their peaks cutting into the sky. For Dave, the hills and mountains had always felt like old friends keeping him company on the journey, and it meant a mixture of melancholy and nostalgia whenever he made the trip.

"You know, Lennie..." he began, glancing over at his half-awake son, whose head was resting against the window, eyes half-closed from the long drive. "...I wasn't always, shall we say, a businessman."

His son stirred slightly, blinking as he processed the words. The idea of his father being anything other than the man he knew now was hard to imagine. "What do you mean?" the boy asked, his voice drowsy but curious, the question hanging in the air between them.

"I used to be a teacher," said Dave. "Before your mom and I moved up to Maine, I taught at an elementary school in Newton, close to where your mom lives now. But I quit."

For a moment, Lennie tried imagining his father sitting at the front of a classroom, correcting homework and handing out assignments, like his own first-grade teacher. "Dad..." he asked suspiciously, "...are you lying?"

"No way!" said Dave. "Go ahead, ask your mother when you go back to Massachusetts."

Lennie considered things for a moment. His dad was certainly capable of messing with him, and he wondered if perhaps this was the case now. Still, his dad's imagination was just as good as the truth, and so he inquired further. "What happened? Why'd you quit teaching and come here to run the sauna? And why didn't mom come too?"

"That's a lot of questions." Dave paused allowing him some time to figure out just how he was going to navigate through this adult subject matter.

The truth was, he hadn't exactly quit. In the end, he had been fired after making the simple, common-sense decision to give one of his students a ride home... on his motorcycle. While he enjoyed teaching kids, Dave knew the firing was probably for the best. By the end of his tenure, he had already realized that, in the long run, there was very little chance he could successfully navigate the school's politics and rules. After all, most of them went against the way he wanted to live his life.

It was also true that Dave's first wife, Rachel, had come with him to Maine, but his inability to keep his impulses in check eventually drove her back to Massachusetts, taking Lennie with her. Wanting to maintain his image as the hero, however, Dave wasn't about to share the full story with his son.

"The school had a lot of rules, and I've just never been very good at following them," he said, steering the conversation away from the truth. "I had my own unique teaching methods. Like, sometimes I'd bring animals into the classroom, or take my students on unique field trips."

All of this sounded marvelous to Lennie, who had just completed his first year of school. "Your mom - " Dave continued, "...she did come with me. But it turns out this way of living just wasn't for her." This made sense to the boy, who struggled to picture his mother in anything but a crisp white button-down blouse and a pair of heels.

"Before I stopped teaching, we started making trips up to Maine, looking at land for sale. On our third trip, we found ourselves traveling up a long, bumpy dirt road leading to a small piece of land that just felt like the right fit." Dave shared the memory with a warmth in his voice. "It was cheap, and your mother liked the spot. So... we figured we'd give it a shot!"

"Was I born yet?" asked Lennie.

"No, this was still before your time kid. We didn't even have a house for our first six months. We just camped out in a tent on the land." For a moment Dave flashed back almost a decade. "But with some help from our neighbors, we were able to build a small house to live in!" he continued, with enthusiasm. "And we did most of the work naked!" he said proudly.

Lennie laughed at the thought of this. Now here was something the young boy could easily picture. His dad loved to be naked, and he displayed no shame or hesitation about it. "Wait!" said the boy working to put the pieces of this story together in his own mind. "Are you talking about mom's shed? The one she keeps here in Maine?"

Dave nodded his head. During their divorce settlement, his ex-wife had been granted half of the property, including the piece of their land where their original dwelling sat. After they had first split, Rachel would often come up for weekends with her girlfriends.

Her ex-husband, who was still experiencing bitterness from the divorce settlement, would use this as an opportunity to sneak over and hide rotten meat under the porch.

"Yeah, that was it." Dave leaned forward and tuned the radio, sparing his son the additional detail.

"Can you turn it up?" asked Lennie "I like this song.

———

After about an hour more of driving, a sign reading *Welcome to New Hampshire – Live Free or Die* appeared on the right side of the road.

"They must be talking about us!" said Dave, cranking the volume up. A few minutes later, they pulled into a parking lot behind a small convenience store in the small town of Gorham, New Hampshire. Dave carefully backed his truck up to a bulkhead that led to the basement of the building, before he and Lennie climbed out of the truck.

They carefully stepped onto a set of old concrete steps and headed down into a cool and dingy basement where they were hit with a strong musky stench and cigar smoke. The basement was poorly lit by a lamp sitting on a folding table over in the corner, where four large men sat with poker chips and cash piled high on the table. Only one of the men turned to look at the newcomers.

"Hey Dave, let me just finish this hand," said Tony, who was the storeowner. "I'm about to own Jeb's farm!" he said, smiling at the guy sitting across from him. "Not that I'd want it,' he stated. "Now if he'd throw in his wife…" he suggested to the other men at the table, before trailing his voice off.

The store owner had an accent and a stature that reminded Dave of every Italian tough guy portrayed in the movies. But for the most part, he was a normal guy who had bought the convenience store almost thirty years ago, and Dave's visits were the closest he got to ever being a benevolent crime boss. "Grab a beer if you're thirsty" he offered, pointing to a large cooler on his right.

Turning to Lennie he continued, pointing in the direction of a second set of stairs, mostly hidden behind a pile of empty boxes. "Hey kid, go ahead and grab yourself a root beer upstairs,"

Lennie, who was always happy to access the sugar high that his dad usually denied him, quickly obliged, and bounded up the stairs.

———

Nancy eyed the unusual man sitting at the bar, intrigued by his odd behavior. As she watched him, he fished out another pickle from a jar with his large fingers and proceeded to slather it with peanut butter using a white plastic butter knife. After licking the knife, he devoured the entire thing in one bite. Grateful that she'd recently overcome the morning sickness of her first trimester, Nancy tucked her drying rag into the front pocket of her apron and walked over in his direction.

Rob had been renting one of the rooms above the sauna for a few months now. With a brownish-red beard, large eyes, and flip flops, he resembled a younger, less hygienic Santa Claus. As far as Nancy could tell, his favorite pastime seemed to be staring off into the abyss.

Despite his eccentricities, both Dave and Nancy liked him. He always paid his rent on time, helped mostly by some disability payment he received monthly. And though he didn't seem particularly skilled in any notable way, he was always ready to lend a hand whenever he was around—which, as it turned out, was often. He had introduced himself simply as Rob, but his peculiar habits quickly earned him the extended nickname *Weird Rob*.

"And I thought I was having some strange cravings lately," Nancy said jokingly and clearing away a couple of empty beer cans next to him.

"Really?" Weird Rob replied hopefully, missing her tone completely. "Like what?" he inquired as he continued licking the sticky peanut butter and pickle juice from his fingers. After satisfying himself, he slowly started rubbing his nipples in circles.

Nancy pulled the dish rag from her apron pocket and snapped it at him. "No, not like that!" she rebuked him. "Get your mind right with Jesus. I was talking about your…culinary choices!

"Hey now, don't shoot it down until you've given it a try!" he insisted. "I should know, I've tried just about everything," he admitted with not hint of shame.

With a bemused smile, Nancy turned to look at the clock on the wall. She was hoping that Dave and Lennie would be getting back soon. She had already spent all morning on her feet at the diner, only to come home and discover that her husband had taken his son with him on one of his beer runs. This of course meant that she was left to start the fires and make the pizzas, and by now she was both tired and a little pissed.

"Hey Nancy…" came Weird Rob's voice from the end of the bar. "Do you know where the hot sauce packets I had in here?" he asked holding a white and blue ceramic vase upside down and shaking it.

"No idea!" Nancy said without looking in the direction of the tenant. She let her hands roam over her growing belly and thought for a moment about the baby inside. She was grateful that she and Dave's living situation had been upgraded from sleeping on the sauna floor to living in one of the small apartments upstairs. But with her first child on the way, she dreamed of more, wanting a home away from the sauna and its pickle and peanut butter eating tenants. She guessed that, for now, she was simply going to have to fake it for a while.

Just then, Lennie and Dave burst through the front door, carrying cases of beer, like hunters returning with their kills for the tribe. "Back here, buddy, behind the bar," his dad instructed. His son followed him behind the counter and stacked his load onto the cases that his dad had just set on the floor.

"You're back!" Nancy called out.

"What gave it away?" Dave joked.

"I'm hungry!" Lennie chimed in, eager to draw attention to his empty stomach.

"Hang on. I've got a casserole in the oven!" Nancy said with encouragement as the young boy jumped on one of the bar stools.

"Not until we unload the truck," Dave insisted, a firm hand landing on his son's shoulder, and the boy reluctantly headed back outside with his dad.

Before they began unloading, Dave paused and turned to Lennie, a glint of mischief in his eyes. "Hey Lennie, what do I always tell you?"

The young boy knew exactly what was coming. A grin spread across his face, and with practiced enthusiasm, he responded, "Liquor licenses are for suckers!"

His father's face lit up, a proud grin spreading across his features. "You got it kid!"

CHAPTER 5

HUSBANDS AND WIVES, BUT RARELY TOGETHER

"Mothers, fathers, black and white,
women with women, always my favorite sight
There were bikers and teachers and sins of desire,
when winter came there was even a fire
There were hippies and rednecks and local Norwegians
Rastas, Russians, and even some vegans"

(1980)

Thursday evenings at the sauna were typically quieter than weekends, and tonight was no exception. After the family finished a late dinner of crockpot beef stew, Dave settled into his usual spot by the fireplace. Aside from the crackling fire and the rhythmic tapping and clicking of Weird Rob, who was tinkering with a pair of old magnets at the bar, everything was peaceful. Dave closed his eyes, pretending to sleep, while he listened to Nancy quietly switching out the laundry in the back.

The calm was soon interrupted by the roar of a motorcycle pulling up outside. Dave assumed it was one of the bikers from the local motorcycle club, and with a reluctant sigh, he pushed himself out of his chair and went behind the counter to grab a couple of beers. As he turned, the front door swung open, and he was pleasantly surprised to see two women in their twenties—both dressed in leather jackets, tight jeans, and high leather boots.

One of the bikers sported a mullet and had finely sculpted, androgynous features that made her resemble a feminine version of

Michael J. Fox. The other had a mostly shaven head, with a single wave of golden curls that she kept brushing away from her piercing blue eyes. As Dave watched with amusement, they sauntered confidently up to the bar.

"You girls from around here?" he asked enthusiastically.

With a playful grin, the woman with the golden curls replied, "Do we *look* like we're from around here?"

Her friend chipped in, "Folks we know in Portland told us about this place. They said it's always a good time!"

Dave felt their eyes on him and, eager to impress, he straightened up. "Well, you've found the right spot! We know how to have fun around here. I can get a sauna ready for you if you'd like."

"Actually…" the biker with the mullet interjected, "…can we just chill for now." Her companion nodded in agreement. "You know, have a beer, play some pool… maybe put our name down for a later slot?"

"Sure thing!" Dave replied. "What's your name?"

"Trouble!" the woman with the blue eyes said, a wicked smile playing at the corners of her lips.

Dave grinned and reached into one of the coolers, grabbed a couple of PBRs, and handed each of the women a can. As they walked toward the pool table, he admired how well their tight jeans fit the curves of their bodies.

"Hey, Rob! Throw on some tunes, will ya?" Dave called over to his tenant.

Weird Rob looked up from his magnets and gave an enthusiastic thumbs up, just as a familiar face walked through the door.

"Hey, brother! You got running water at your place yet?" Dave greeted Saul who was wearing his usual dirty overalls, and barely concealing a bong tucked under his coat. It reminded him of Tommy Chong from *Up in Smoke*, that he and Nancy had just caught at the Bridgton drive-in just a few weeks ago.

"Not yet," his buddy answered, scratching his head. "But I had an excavator out last weekend to dig for the septic tank I'm finally putting in." He grinned proudly, clearly pleased with his progress. "I was happy enough with the outhouse, but you know how it is with women…" He trailed off, his voice betraying the strain of his own personal struggles.

Saul shifted uneasily, his hands fumbling with the brim of his worn baseball cap as if the action could help ease his discomfort. He had always been a man of few words when it came to his personal life, but there was no mistaking the hint of frustration in his tone. "It's just… sometimes, you try to do things the right way, and it never feels like enough."

Dave could feel for his friend. He was the kind of guy who was thoughtful and considerate—everything women said they wanted—but his lack of alpha-male swagger, combined with his indifference to personal hygiene, kept him in the dreaded friend zone. As a result, his love life was practically nonexistent.

"Oh, you'll get there," Dave offered in support, hoping his words would eventually prove true.

"I trust the universe." Saul said with a hopeful grin. "And until then, at least I get to see you every week!" He brightened a little.

"Works for me," Dave replied. He noticed his friends gaze had already shifted over to the two women at the pool table. "One towel or two?" he asked, purely out of habit. He knew his friend well enough to guess that one towel would be more than enough—and that Saul would only use it as a cold compress to extend his time in the sauna.

"Oh, just one, please!" Saul said, clearly eager to get on with it but not without a little reluctance.

Dave grabbed a single towel from the bar and handed it to his buddy. "You're in room fourteen,"

Saul groaned in response, clearly not thrilled with the news. That room was at the end of the line and the sauna's makeshift hot water system, cobbled together over the years, didn't have the reserves to handle the needs of a sauna business. The result was that customers in the farther rooms often ended up with cold plunges. If anyone complained, Dave would spin some half-true spiel about the *true Finnish tradition* of alternating between hot saunas and cold plunges.

"Sorry, man. That's just how it is tonight," Dave said, casually brushing it off. "It's a slow night, and Nancy didn't get many fires going today. Plus, she picked the wrong rooms. You can grab a bucket of kindling on your way in, though."

"I'll do that," Saul replied, making a mental note to grab a couple of buckets. He knew how his buddy liked to skimp on wood during the slow times, barely keeping the stoves burning. If he was going to be stuck with cold water, he'd at least make sure the room was hot enough to tolerate it.

As his friend walked away, Dave offered up something to help balance the scales. "Hey, you don't mind some company, do you?" he asked, gesturing back to the two women at the pool table.

It wouldn't be the first time Dave had attempted to use his powers as sauna master to match strangers into a room together. In fact, he viewed his direct intervention as a charitable endeavor, patting himself on the back every time the successful results were loudly broadcast.

A look of delight came over Saul's face. "No, I definitely do *not* mind company. Just let them know I'm quite comfortable with nudity. It would probably be best if they were as well," he said with a trace of hopeful anticipation in his voice.

"I'll see what I can do," said Dave giving his friend a nudge. And with that, Saul happily headed down the hall.

Dave returned to his chair and contemplated his best approach for the task in front of him. The two guests were now alternating between playing pool and dancing suggestively to the Eagles Greatest

Hits eight track tape that Weird Rob had popped in.

Around the corner Nancy emerged from the hallway with a basket full of freshly cleaned towels in her arms. "Hey David," she said, breaking his focus. "Don't forget. It's Lennie's birthday Saturday."

Dave glanced over at his wife. "Nancy, I would never forget my son's birthday," her husband stated firmly.

Nancy rolled her eyes and dumped out the towels onto the counter. She knew full well that was exactly what he had done.

"Be there and love them. That's all they need. And don't forget to teach them what real fucking work is!" he added.

"And you gotta have at least a couple in case something happens to one…" said Nancy before finishing his mantra mockingly with "…you've got others!"

Dave was impressed. Even a little turned on. He picked up a towel off the bar and began to fold it. "You know Nancy… this year, to celebrate…I'm only going to make him load six barrels of kindling this weekend instead of the usual eight!"

There it was. Nancy shook her head. "Come on David, you better do something fun with him this year. Not simply take him on another one of your beer runs to New Hampshire!"

"Hey, we needed more beer. Besides he loved doing that. I even let him drive!" her husband said proudly.

"You probably did," Nancy replied with a suspicious tone in her voice, refolding the very same towel that Dave had just finished with.

"I already folded that towel!" he said, feeling a little annoyed at her oversight. He was Lennie's father. She was the boy's stepmother. He could do whatever he wanted with his son.

"Sorry David, it's just that —" he cut her off.

"I folded that towel just fine!" he insisted as his voice grew louder and angrier.

"David, please!" Nancy said gesturing to Weird Rob at the bar and the two ladies dancing and playing pool. She didn't want to get into a public dispute with him like this.

Dave lowered his voice. "You always do this kind of thing. I'm not an idiot and I know how to do the fucking laundry. And I think I know when my own goddamn son's birthday is!" His voice was harsh and antagonistic.

Nancy was taken aback, and her eyes began to water. Maybe she should have gone easier on her husband. She knew how difficult it was for him to only see his son on a limited basis.

Dave's bruised ego didn't have the patience for much more. He glanced at the clock. "I'm going to still need to be here for another couple hours," he said gruffly. "Why don't you go up to bed?" It wasn't really a suggestion, and Nancy knew it. Since she was already rundown from her day, she simply stripped off her apron and made her way up the stairs to the second floor.

Dave exhaled deeply. He wasn't fooling himself. He really had forgotten all about Lennie's birthday. And truthfully, he couldn't fold towels as meticulously as Nancy did. Details like that just didn't matter to him. But fuck, she should just be grateful that he even tried, right?

Dave reached down behind the bar, grabbed a PBR and cracked it open. He didn't usually drink his own cheap shit but tonight seemed like a night for making bad decisions. He took a sip of the piss warm beer and turned in the direction of the ladies at the pool table. At least now he was free to carry on with the evening in whatever manner he pleased.

This meant abandoning the half-folded laundry and his plans to hook Saul up. Instead, he headed back in the direction of the newcomers, with his beer. "Are you ladies ready for your sauna? It's on the house tonight if you don't mind sharing," the sauna owner said smiling.

The two young women looked at each other and then back over at Dave. "I suppose you could join us," said the blonde. "I'm Bonnie and this is my girlfriend, Jade."

———

With the full approval of the group secured now, he took the ladies down the corridor and into a changing room. "Kind of a small room," said Jade, looking inside the closet like space. "Give us a few minutes to settle in first."

Only slightly disappointed, Dave respectfully agreed and headed back towards the lounge area hearing giggles as they closed the door behind him.

"Hey Rob! Do you remember how to close up?" he asked his tenant, who was busy in the small kitchen area making himself an egg sandwich.

"Of course, Dave — I'm not an idiot!" Weird Rob replied. "Just let me get this toast out of the toaster," he said, brandishing a fork.

Dave pulled the plug out from the wall and continued. "Put the towels from the washer into the dryer. Hose down everything. Lock the front door…and don't loiter outside my sauna room too long." He gave him a wink.

"Changing room is all yours!" came a voice from down the hall.

"Good luck!" Weird Rob offered.

Stepping into the dressing room, Dave caught sight of a pair of white panties hanging on the wall hook and he took a moment to run his fingers through them. He quickly got undressed and let his shirt and shorts fall into a crumpled pile on the floor. Not wanting to go into the sauna room too eager, he paused and made a concentrated effort to relax his most exposed parts before entering.

Inside, he respectfully took a seat on the far end of the wooden bench that the two women were occupying. He watched in quiet appreciation as they took turns massaging each other with some of the sauna's peppermint soap. Soon Bonnie, whom Dave suspected was the driver of the bike parked outside, had her eyes closed and was surrendering into the bolder and bolder hands of Jade.

With his hand resting on his rigid cock, Dave caught the eyes of Jade. She had a wicked grin across her face making it evident of her appreciation for a viewing audience. It was clear that he had indeed read the room right.

But he understood the rules. *Stay quiet, keep his hands to himself, and do not even think about ejaculating anywhere near them.*

CHAPTER 6

WHO IS GOING TO SAVE THIS MAINER'S SOUL?

"I didn't move here for conflict
So, stop trying to push me away
Maine is not my Vacation
And brother I think that I'll stay"

(1980)

Nancy sat alone in the family apartment, nestled just above the sauna lounge, nursing her newborn son, Walter. It was Dave's second time around as a father, and he wasn't feeling the same level of stress that his first son's birth had provided. But for Nancy, it was all new, and she had been blindsided by the physical and emotional challenges of new motherhood. The labor had stretched over two days, and now, sitting in the aftermath, she felt like a deflated balloon—sore and engorged, struggling to adjust.

To make matters worse, she kept swinging between overwhelming love for her baby and a deep sense of loneliness. And Walter—tiny and fragile—seemed to cry constantly. *I don't remember Lennie crying this much*, Dave had told her only a few hours ago. The comparison stung. She didn't want him to see Walter as just a continuation of his first-born son. And eight years had passed since Lennie was a newborn; what could Dave possibly remember from that time anyway?

As she leaned down to inhale the sweet scent of her baby's head, the familiar Saturday evening bustle downstairs reached her ears—a mix of locals and out-of-state skiers visiting for the weekend. For nearly five years, Nancy had been the one running around, making pizzas and juggling tasks on nights like this. But now, with a newborn, it was Dave who was handling it all on his own, with only Saul—who helped occasionally—and their tenant, Weird Rob, around to lend a hand. *Three grown men should be able to manage*, she thought, though she had little faith in that.

Suddenly, a sharp crash and a gasp echoed from below—broken glass. Nancy recognized the sound from her years in the service industry. *Perfect. Something to keep him busy*, she thought. Resisting the urge to check, she adjusted the ice pack under her and settled back into her bed to resume nursing Walter.

As she shifted the baby onto her other breast, She heard her husband's voice, followed by a woman's high-pitched laugh. The sound sliced through the quiet of the room, and Nancy froze. She tried to refocus on Walter, but the loneliness was even more pronounced than before. The laughter echoed in her mind, uninvited and sharp, invading the space between her and the life she was trying to build with Dave.

She shifted uncomfortably, and in that moment, a painful truth settled in. She wasn't prepared in any way—physically or emotionally—to keep up with Dave. She had expected it be hard after the baby, but this... this felt like something different. She knew how skilled her husband was at charming women—he had done it with her, after all. Turning on the charm effortlessly, weaving his way into the hearts of strangers with a smile.

But the thought of him betraying their marriage, especially now with a newborn in the picture, was too much for her to handle. She pushed the thought aside, swallowing the knot in her throat, and refusing to let it take root in her mind.

She closed her eyes for a moment and focused on her son. In that moment, everything felt fragile, like it could crumble at the slightest touch. She wasn't sure what tomorrow would bring, but for now, she'd stay in her own small world, the quiet rhythm of Walter nursing offering her a small, temporary solace.

———

Downstairs, the lounge had descended into a noisy chaos. "Rob!" Dave called across the room. "Where'd the broom and dustpan go?"

"I'm just finishing up in sauna three's changing room," came Weird Rob's voice from down the hall. "You can have them in a minute."

Dave sighed, looking over at a woman kneeling on the floor, picking up shards of broken glass.

"I'm so sorry!" she said with a thick Boston accent. "I brought a beer in with me and —"

"No worries," Dave said, bending down to help her. "I own this place, and pretty girls like you cause more damage than this on a regular basis. That's why I only sell cans!"

The woman smiled at him, brushing a strand of long brown hair behind her ear. Dave sensed the opening and leaned in. "So, what brings you here tonight?"

She blushed. "I was supposed to meet an old college friend here, but her kid's sick, so she bailed. I didn't want to stay cooped up in my motel room. She turned her gaze to him. "So, I thought I'd go out for a little adventure by myself!"

"I see," Dave said quickly, sensing an opportunity. "And have you found one yet?"

She shook her head and sighed. "Not yet, I'm afraid."

"What's your name?" he continued.

"Rebecca," she said, offering her hand.

"Rebecca…" Dave repeated, taking her hand in his own. "… ever party before?"

"Party?" she asked with a small laugh. "What do you mean?"

Dave glanced around the room, before leaning in and slightly, lowering his voice. "You know… party?" he said, touching the side of his nose and giving a subtle sniff.

"Oh…" Rebecca grinned, embarrassed but amused. "I get it."

The moment was disrupted when Weird Rob appeared. "Here you go!" he said, abruptly shoving a broom in Dave's face, oblivious to the negotiation currently underway.

Dave reluctantly took it, eyeing his tenant's back pocket. "Are those… panties?".

"Yup…found them in one of the rooms. Finders' keepers!" Weird Rob said smugly, before turning to Rebecca. "Your sauna's all set now, miss."

Rebecca's face fell slightly.

"Um… okay," she said, uncertain how to proceed. "Is there a trash somewhere I could use first?"

"There's a bathroom down the hall," Weird Rob clarified, eager to get away.

"I've got it," Dave said, holding out the dustpan. "Just put it here, and I'll bring you a replacement for your sauna, if you're interested?" he offered, hoping to regain some momentum.

Rebecca hesitated, but before she could respond, the front door swung open, and a voice bellowed from across the room.

"Dave!"

Dave looked up to see his neighbor marching toward him, clearly agitated.

"We need to talk!" he barked, his face was puffy and red.

Dave's pulse quickened. "What about?" he asked innocently.

The neightbor leaned in close. "You know very well what this is about!" he said through gritted teeth.

Dave laughed nervously. "Oh, come on, neighbor, calm down. Whatever it is, it can't be that bad."

The neighbor thrust a piece of a broken pine branch toward Dave's face. "You cut down my tree!"

"What?" Dave feigned surprise. "That tree? It was on my

property. I couldn't find the pins, but the deed says it was on mine. I didn't want it falling on the building during a storm."

His neighbor gave him a hurt look. "That tree wouldn't have fallen near your building, and whatever deed you're referring to isn't the one I know. You can't just go cutting down trees on someone else's property."

"Well, what's done is done," Dave said dismissively. "It was looking ready to go, anyway."

His neighbor was having none of it. "That's not the point, Dave! You can't just do whatever you want!"

Dave put an arm around his shoulders, trying to defuse the tension. "Look, in the future, I'll check in with you before doing anything questionable near our border, okay? Want a drink? A sauna? A sauna with your wife? Or maybe one with someone else?" He winked suggestively.

The neighbor yanked away, disgusted. "There's not a chance in hell you'll ever see me or my wife in one of your saunas. I'm tired of you and your patrons acting like you own the place—smoking weed in the parking lot, urinating on my lawn, and..." He leaned in closer. "...having sex in public, in your cars, right out there!"

Dave smirked. "Come on, You really think God would approve of you watching that kind of stuff? You'd have to be *trying* to see it."

The neighbor flushed with embarrassment and turned pale as he realized the implications of his own words. He stood silently for a moment, then declared, "This is it, Dave. No more chances. Next time, I'm going straight to the cops!"

"You sure about that?" Dave teased. "Might be a shorter drive then you imagined," he said, gesturing to an off-duty member of the Paris Police Department who was busy playing pool."

The neighbor shook his head and stormed back out the door.

Dave turned back to continue his conversation with Rebecca, only to find she had already disappeared into her sauna. Disappointed, he headed back to the bar, where Saul was tossing pizzas.

"What's up with that guy tonight?" Saul asked, suppressing a laugh.

"Oh, him?" Dave chuckled. "He's just... different."

"Yeah," Saul agreed, reaching for the red sauce. "But seriously, what'd you do this time?"

"Nothing!" his friend protested.

Saul wasn't convinced.

"Okay, fine. I may have *technically* cut down a tree that was on his property," he admitted.

Saul shook his head. "Why do you always have to mess with him?"

"I don't mean to... well, not *always*," Dave said. "But he's always looking for something to complain about."

Saul slid a pizza over to a couple at the end of the bar and Dave's eyes drifted over to Weird Rob, currently sniffing the panties he'd found in the sauna.

"Jesus Rob! Get a fucking room!

———

The next morning, Dave descended the stairs early and settled into his chair. *That tree was blocking the sunlight*, he thought, letting out a satisfied sigh.

CHAPTER 7

BREAKFAST AT THE COUNTRY WAY

"Now I've got three kids money buried somewhere
And I'm doing my best to hide the grays in my hair
I don't ask for much, but maybe I should
I just want some attention like he gives to his wood"

(1982)

The early morning light filtered through the small kitchen window above the old drop-in sink at the farm. Dave, already sweaty from working outdoors, stood at the sink refilling his mason jar. After topping it off, he leaned against the counter and gulped most of it down, savoring the taste as he watched the sun come up. Before coming to Maine, he'd never given much thought to water. But he'd quickly discovered just how special it was in Maine, especially when it came from your own well.

Now that he was having a bit of financial success and with a growing family, Dave had moved them to a white farmhouse and barn on 500 acres along Route 26 in West Paris, just a short drive from the sauna. The space was a welcome change, with more room to spread out and multiple bedrooms—plus, it offered some distance from his sauna clientele. It was perfect timing, too, with Lennie visiting for the summer and bringing along two of his school friends, all of whom were still asleep upstairs. After taking one last gulp of water, he put the jar back in the sink, and headed back outside.

Upstairs, Nancy awoke to the sound of the door closing below.

She remained still next to their youngest son, trying to settle the queasiness in her stomach. Pregnant again and nearing the end of her first trimester, she knew she had a limited window to get to the bathroom before things were likely to get messy. But she was hoping to avoid waking the baby—she didn't want to commit to hours of breastfeeding when there remained the possibility of getting a few more minutes of sleep.

It wasn't going to be easy. The infant was a restless sleeper and was now sprawled across the middle of the bed, arms and legs flung out in every direction. Nancy carefully inched away from him and allowed her pillow to take her place, hoping it would be enough.

Her toes were almost touching the floor, before Walter let out a soft groan and shifted in his sleep. She froze, holding her breath. The little boy reached out for something and, after finding the pillow, settled back into a deep sleep. Nancy tiptoed out of the room, down the creaky stairs, and into the bathroom just off the kitchen. She closed the door behind her and let out a quiet sigh of relief. For the time being, the early morning was still hers.

After finishing in the bathroom, Nancy entered the kitchen, lit a match, and turned the gas stove's knob. After a few clicks, the burner flared to life. She set the kettle on the stove, placed an empty teacup on the counter, and listened. She could hear Dave working outside, and she knew that in a few minutes, a very sweaty, very hungry man would come through that door, expecting the smell of bacon and a hearty breakfast.

She also knew that soon enough there would also be three young boys ready to eat. And while she loved her stepson, Nancy wished Dave had talked to her first before extending an invitation to two of Lennie's friends, BJ and Brendan, to stay for the summer. Her husband was hoping it would help keep Lennie happy and, more importantly, provide him with some free labor. For weeks now, he'd kept them busy with all sorts of Maine activities, like splitting and stacking wood. But it was still a lot of extra work for a pregnant woman with a one-year-old.

As the kettle began to boil, Nancy turned off the burner, hoping the whistling hadn't woken anyone upstairs. She paused and listened for signs of movement. Hearing none, she added a teabag to her cup and took a seat at the small wooden kitchen table. A few more minutes of peace would be a gift before the chaos of breakfast began.

Just as she began to settle in, Dave walked through the screen door shirtless, his voice teasing as he entered. "What, no bacon this morning?" His tone was disappointed but playful, his sweaty body glistening in the early light like a Greek god.

"I was getting there, David," Nancy replied, lifting her head from the table where it had been resting.

Dave gave her a sympathetic look. "Not feeling well?"

"It's just morning sickness," Nancy sighed. "I thought I was over it, but I can feel it coming on. I haven't thrown up yet, but I hoped it'd be best to move slow."

Dave opened the refrigerator, peering inside. "Well, I could do the cooking!" he offered enthusiastically, trying to make up for his earlier sarcastic remark. "Oh, wait…" He sighed in disappointment. "We're out of bacon… and eggs… and orange juice…"

At that moment, a high-pitched wail from upstairs cut through the conversation—Walter was awake.

"Your youngest is up," Nancy stood up quickly and headed upstairs.

Dave, caving to his hunger pains, sighed. "Just get him dressed, and I'll wake up the boys. We're going to the Country Way!"

———

"I'm getting waffles!" BJ shouted from the back of the truck as they pulled into the Country Way parking lot.

"I'm getting French toast!" Brendan declared proudly.

Lennie, sitting on a spare tire in the truck bed, thought for a moment. "I'm not sure what I'm getting," he said. "But I'm hungry enough to eat a horse!"

"A horse, Lennie? Really?" Dave caught the exchange as he climbed out of the driver's seat.

"I mean it, Dad!" Lennie called out. "After all the work we did yesterday, I'm starving!"

"Okay, okay," Dave said, grinning. "Let's make things interesting, then."

"How?" Brendan asked.

"No, David!" Nancy interjected with a warning tone as she worked to get Walter out of his car-seat.

"Oh yes!" Dave grinned at the boys. "Saturdays at the Country Way are all-you-can-eat. So, here's the challenge: whoever can eat the most - "

"David, please! My stomach can't take this," Nancy begged.

"... gets the afternoon off from stacking wood at the sauna," Dave finished, ignoring Nancy's plea.

The boys cheered, setting off an angry cry from Walter, who had awakened from his slumber.

The kids rushed across the parking lot towards the restaurant. "Slow down!" Dave shouted after them, but the boys were already halfway to the door. "Knuckleheads!"

A few minutes later, the family was seated in a booth at the back of the restaurant. Nancy's old co-worker, Betsy, came over with paper placemats and crayons. "Well, if it isn't the whole gang!" she said with a smile. "What can I get you all to drink?"

"We'll all have orange juice," Dave replied, glancing at Nancy for confirmation. "And tea for Nancy."

"You got it!" Betsy said. "The buffet's ready whenever you are."

The boys needed no encouragement. They charged toward the buffet, scanning the offerings: bacon, sausage, ham, scrambled eggs, pancakes, waffles, French toast, crepes, fresh fruit, whipped cream, and berries. It was almost too much to take in, and they enthusiastically dove in, filling their plates with as much food as their plate could carry.

Less than fifteen minutes later, their initial enthusiasm had waned, and they began dragging their feet between trips to the buffet. Meanwhile, Dave kept up his commentary, loud enough for everyone in the restaurant to hear. "Hey Lennie, just letting you know, you're three pieces of toast and a glass of orange juice behind your buddies!"

Lennie groaned, but he had no intention of backing down. Not only was he hoping to avoid an afternoon of splitting wood, but he was determined to earn his father's approval. He took a deep breath and got up from the table. "Order me another juice, Dad," he said, slowly making his way to the buffet, his stomach in full protest mode.

He returned to the table with another plate of toast and quietly promised himself that if he could just clear his plate, he would never eat again.

Nancy, watching with concern, decided it was time to intervene. "Look at him!" she scolded Dave, nodding toward his oldest son.

"What?" Dave asked. "They're just having fun! You wouldn't get it."

"You're right, David. I don't get it! And I certainly don't approve," Nancy said, standing up from the table. "I'm getting the check."

As she made her way toward the register, Lennie's face grew green with nausea. As Betsy set down a fresh glass of juice she offered her thoughts. "You don't look so hot, sweetie," she said.

"I'm good," he replied weakly. Unconvinced, the waitress shook her head and walked away.

"Who's in the lead, Dad?" Lennie asked, trying to change the subject.

"I am!" Brendan groaned from across the table, looking

miserable.

"Barely though," Dave said, grinning. "Lennie, if you can finish that toast and juice, you win!"

Lennie stared at the plate. He knew he was at a crossroads. Stop now and lose or push through and win his father's favor. He decided to push onward and wearily bit into a piece of toast. He immediately regretted it, as he felt the inevitable rising to the surface.

Dave noticed his son's pale face and realized what was about to happen. He slid out of the booth, picked his son up, threw him over his shoulder, and raced for the door.

As they passed the tables, Lennie fought to hold back the deluge. "Hang in there!" Dave encouraged his son. But Lennie's stomach rebelled and just as they reached the door, a flood of vomit erupted. It splashed across the carpet and all over the register, where Nancy was trying to pay the bill.

Dave, who still carrying his son, turned to the cashier and improvised. "Is everyone in the kitchen keeping their hands clean?" he joked. "I think we've got food poisoning here," he stated definitively as he hurried out the door.

———

Once outside, Dave was unable to contain himself and he burst into a fit of laughter. Lennie was still trying to wrap his mind around what had just happened, but his dad's happiness was infectious, and he quickly joined in. As they laughed together, it felt like time had slowed down, and the moment might last forever.

A few minutes later, The rest of the family finally emerged from the chaos inside. Nancy's posture spoke volumes, and it was clear who had done the cleanup. After securing the baby in his car seat, she climbed into the truck without saying a word, and her eyes remained fixated out the front window.

Once Dave had managed to regain his composure, he leaned over the truck bed and cleared his throat, ready to make his final ruling.

"Unfortunately, Lennie," he said with a mock serious tone, "you've been disqualified due to the puking. If you'd just held it until we got outside, I might've let it slide, but I can't. BJ wins the all-you-can-eat contest."

BJ let out a loud cheer and Brendan playfully slapped him on the back. Lennie was not thrilled with the outcome, but he knew better than to argue. He was, after all, living in his dad's world.

And it was a small price to pay for such an epic story.

BREAKFAST AT THE COUNTRY WAY

CHAPTER 8

DUPING TAPES – GIMME A BREAK

"The FBI they wanted me
On this of course we all agree
But duping tapes gimme a break
I've sold more drugs than they can make"

(1983)

"I need you to finish unloading that wood when we get back to the sauna," Dave reminded his oldest son, nodding to the back of the pickup truck.

"Can't I eat something first?" Lennie pleaded as he slumped over in the passenger seat. The excitement of the long work hours with his dad was fading fast. Already that day, they had spent a couple hours splitting wood on the farm, and now they were returning from a two-hour round trip from Falmouth, where they had delivered half of the load.

"I already got you out of babysitting this morning," Dave said, glancing at his son. "Just take care of this first, then you can eat."

Lennie sighed, and as they passed the new McDonald's in downtown Paris, he found himself daydreaming of a cheeseburger.

As Dave made his turn into the gravel parking lot of the sauna, he noticed a black sedan following closely. It was too early for customers—and most of them drove pick-ups or VW buses. Even the out-of-staters didn't typically drive sedans. His gut tightened. Something felt off.

Lennie saw his dad looking in the rear-view mirror. "Who's that,

Dad?"

Dave didn't answer. "Stay in the truck, son," he said in a low voice. As he opened his door and stepped out of the vehicle, two well-dressed men in sunglasses got out of the sedan. The men's polished appearance made him uneasy.

"Can I help you?" Dave asked.

"We're looking for a David Graiver," said the shorter, stockier of the two.

"Well, you found him," Dave replied coolly. In his head he was already running through a mental list of his possible misdeeds—was it the beer runs? The taxes? He knew there was a long list of things he could be guilty of.

"I'm Special Agent Roberts with the F.B.I.," the man said, removing his sunglasses. "This is Special Agent Harris." The other man silently scribbled something in a notebook, which only added to Dave's unease.

By now Lennie had grown tired of waiting, and he jumped out of the truck. Dave shot him a look. "Go inside and make a sandwich."

"But I thought you wanted me to—"

"Go inside!" Dave cut him off.

Lennie shrugged and headed inside the building, leaving Dave to face the agents.

"Kids," Dave muttered, trying to lighten the mood. The faces of the agent's remained stoic.

Agent Roberts cleared his throat. "We'd like to talk to you inside."

Dave's mind raced as he couldn't remember whether he had left a stash of cash or a pound of weed anywhere in sight. After doing some quick math he surmised that since the agents hadn't drawn their guns, they probably weren't looking into that particular enterprise of his, and he invited the men to follow him inside.

"Take a seat," Dave said once they were in the lounge area, and he headed to his chair over by the wood stove. But the agents stood, unyielding.

"What can I do for you gentlemen? Looking for a sauna?" he asked, unable to resist.

Agent Roberts stepped forward. "We have information that you're renting bootleg VCR tapes. Unauthorized duplication is a federal offense. You could face jail time and hefty fines."

Dave was stunned. VCR tapes? He'd heard the warnings at the beginning of every video but never thought they'd ever be enforced. Now, with the agents standing in front of him, he needed a plan. He decided that lying offered the best path forward.

"I have no idea what you're talking about," Dave said, forcing confusion into his voice. "I rent rooms, not movies. Who is telling you this?"

But it was true. For years he had been renting out movies he had duplicated using two VCR machines he had connected.

"I'm afraid I can't share that information with you," Agent Roberts replied.

Before the conversation could go any further, Nancy walked in holding grocery bags in one hand and a newborn baby in the other. She was followed by a toddler with limited mobility. "Oh, I'm sorry," she said, putting the grocery bags down on the pool table. "Everything ok?" she asked the room.

"Lennie's upstairs," Dave said, his voice steady. "I'll be up in a moment."

Nancy sensed something was off, but she knew not to press, and she immediately took the kids and headed to the 2nd floor. Once she was gone, Dave turned back to the agents. "If you're looking for adult films, you've got the wrong place. I'm just a sauna guy!"

"Mr. Graiver..." Agent Roberts said in a no-nonsense voice. "Shut down the operation or you'll be arrested. Please don't make us come back."

With that, they turned around and left. Dave remained in his chair and considered his options.

It was bad enough that he was going to have to shut down tape operation. But pledging allegiance to government oversight just made him feel dirty.

———

Grant Roland, owner of the Pit Stop gas station and convenience store, was looking out the store window, and saw his buddy pulling up on his motorcycle. He put down the Sun-Journal sports section and took a bite from his morning blueberry muffin, before brushing the crumbs off the counter.

"Morning, Dave," Grant greeted his friend who ignored his greeting and headed straight for the coffee station in back.

"Coffee first," Dave said, grimacing. "Three kids now. It's killing me."

Grant set down his muffin and gave him a concerned look. "What's going on? You don't even drink coffee!"

"I do today! I need a new way to feed the family. This bootleg tape thing…It's over. The feds came yesterday." Dave dropped the news flatly.

The storeowner's eyes widened. "Shit, man. What happened?"

"Somebody ratted me out!" Dave muttered, taking a tiny sip of his coffee. "This small-town shit's ridiculous."

Grant pushed the dollar back toward Dave. "This one's on the house. You'll figure it out. God works in mysterious ways."

His friend tucked the money in his pocket. "Yeah? What's he got in mind for a law-abiding Jew like me? I was making good cash…I need another idea."

The storeowner leaned forward, lowering his voice. "What about real estate?"

"Selling houses?" Dave raised an eyebrow. "I'm *not* the real-estate type."

Grant grinned. "No, no. Purchasing land. Building rental properties. That's where the money is!" he paused. "I'm doing it myself, just on a small scale," he finished emphatically.

"I've already got the room rentals above the sauna," Dave reminded him.

Grant's enthusiasm grew. "Sure! So, you already know about renting. But think bigger. Land's cheap around here, and I know the ins and outs—plumbing, septic, construction. It's the smart way to go."

Dave mulled it over. "You need a partner?"

Grant slapped the counter. "Exactly. Someone who can think outside the box. You're that guy!"

Dave's mood lifted. "That's what I keep telling my wife!"

———

That night as he lay awake, Dave considered the events from the previous 24 hours. *Time to go big*, he thought to himself. *You can't keep a good Jew down!*"

CHAPTER 9

IF THESE PINE BOARDS COULD TALK

"Husbands and wives but rarely together
and constant remarks about the day's weather
Farmers, and lawyers, off-duty cops, there were
guys who grew veggies and guys who grew pot
Cousins, housewives, and endless betrayals,
loggers, roofers, and even disabled
Mothers, fathers, black and white,
women with women, always my favorite sight"

(1984)

"Really, David? Today?"

It was only 7AM, and Nancy stood at the kitchen counter, preparing peanut butter and jelly sandwiches for what was supposed to be a family beach day.

"Oh, come on, Nance. It's fine. You and the kids can still go and have a good time. I just gotta take care of some business today. And if things go right, you'll be getting more than just a day trip to the ocean," her husband promised.

Nancy turned on the hot water and began washing her cutting board and knife. As the sound of the running water filled the kitchen, she imagined it was some remote tropical waterfall, not the sound of a faucet.

"Hmm," she sighed, her voice tinged with disappointment. She knew that there was no business meeting. It was the local MC renting out the sauna for a private event.

"So, you're telling me that a deal like this could make us, what, *vacation* rich?" she asked skeptically.

"I'm not telling you anything," Dave said, avoiding her gaze. "I just need to be at the sauna today. It's important!" He was in no mood to go over details and was grateful when Lennie came sauntering into the room.

"When are we leaving?" he asked, reaching for a banana from the fruit bowl on the table.

"Your father has some *work* to attend to at the sauna this afternoon," Nancy said sharply. "So, it looks like it's just us and your little brother and sister going to the beach today."

His son paused mid-bite. He was too old to be beach babysitting with his siblings. He looked at his dad, his expression was uncertain. "Well… can I go to the sauna instead?" he asked.

Dave glanced over at his wife, expecting the worse. He was already backing out of the family day. He didn't really imagine her being too excited about losing another member of the team.

But Nancy surprised everyone. "Kid, you're eleven now—old enough to handle it. Have a ball!" She didn't want to be the bad guy; being a stepparent was difficult enough already.

"I'll tell you what…" Dave said, rubbing his hand through his hair. "…you can come with me, but you've gotta understand that you're gonna have to work, keep your head low and mind your business."

Lennie nodded. *That sounds great*, he thought.

"Here," Nancy said handing them each a sandwich before packing the other three away for the beach.

With a not quite free hand, Lennie used the tips of his fingers to slide open the glass door leading out to the small backyard area. The door creaked as it moved, the rusty sound matched well with the rest of the ramshackle atmosphere Dave seemed to love so much.

The backyard itself was modest—a patch of grass dotted with overgrown weeds and a crooked fence that seemed to lean in all directions. Keeping with his usual minimalist theme, the pool that Dave had installed just a few months ago, wasn't much more than a tilled hole in the ground. Sitting next to it was a questionable filtration system that seemed to just barely keep the water from turning mirky and green. The boy, balancing a load of essentials in his arms, stepped cautiously onto hot concrete that surrounded the edges of the pool.

This is a party! he thought. Everywhere he looked people were half naked, some wearing nothing but their leather biker jackets. There were women of all sizes walking around topless, with their breasts ranging from small to very large, on full display. There were tattoos and piercings in places Lennie had never imagined before. Maine's own Jonathan Edwards was blasting from the transistor radio *Gonna lay around the shanty momma and get a good buzz on...* The tinny music, hung in the air, only adding to the odd, laid-back chaos of the scene.

The inground pool itself was packed with at least a dozen local MC members lounging in the cool water and displaying their large beer-bloated bellies. There was a guy sitting on the edge of the shallow end of the pool receiving a blow job. Next to him, on the grass, one of his biker buddies was busy screwing a girl doggy style in full view of amused onlookers.

It was quite a show, and the clutter in his arms was his front row ticket in. Lennie had everything he needed for the circus that was in full swing—warm Nattie Lights, packs of cigarettes, and a half dozen fresh, clean towels that Nancy kept neatly folded and stacked on a shelf behind the makeshift bar.

The young boy made his way around the yard but found no takers for the towels. Giving up the rouse, he simply dropped them in an empty lawn chair sitting in a corner, in case someone developed a sudden shyness. Making his way back around the pool perimeter, he handed out beer and cigarettes, collecting cash in return, and stuffing his pockets with slightly damp dollar bills.

After spending a few minutes picking up a combination of cigarette butts, condoms, and empty nips of alcohol off the ground, Lennie grabbed a Sunkist orange soda and parked himself on top of the picnic table, next to a bowl of potatoes salad. Sharing the table where a couple of bikers fully preoccupied snorting lines of cocaine.

The spot he chose provided him a good spot to keep lookout for his dad and a prime position for viewing all the mayhem. Most importantly for the young boy, it was also where no one would be able to spot his growing excitement.

————

Dave sat at the sauna bar with some of the club's leadership. "I'm telling you this is good quality stuff, coming from the same supplier. Just a different color then we've been working with."

Razor looked at him skeptically. "We already have a sugar supplier down south."

"Exactly!" said Dave. "Don't you think it's time to support local? My source is good and if you work with me, you won't have to risk traveling out of state for pickups."

The conversation continued over the next half hour and as they went back and forth Dave began getting apprehensive. If he closed this deal, it was going to put both him and his buddy Tim in a good position. He needed this to work.

Finally, after settling on numbers, Mac took a hit from the oversized joint being passed around. "Tell you what, we're gonna go out to the pool and try out some of your party favors. If we end up having a good time, then consider it a deal!" he whispered in his soft low voice holding out his hand to seal the deal.

Dave shook Mac's hand and the bikers all headed back out to the party, leaving behind a smiling sauna owner whose breath had finally returned.

————

"Lennie, get your ass in here!" Dave's voice boomed from the sliding door.

Shit, had he missed his dads' entrance? the boy wondered. He grabbed the bowl of potato salad still sitting untouched on the picnic table and held it in front of his crotch as he made his way to the side door.

"Hey Dad, I was just cleaning up back there a bit. I brought you some potato salad?" the boy offered.

"What? No, I need you to go out back and fill fifty buckets of kindlin and six barrels of the big stuff."

"Dad it's eighty-two degrees out!" Lennie replied angrily as he remembered the scene playing out back. "Nobody is going to want to take a sauna today." He had no intention of being pushed out of the picture. And it felt obvious to him that this is exactly what was going on right now.

But the look on his dad's face made it clear that the matter was settled.

This isn't fucking fair! the young boy thought to himself. After all, the sauna was not only the best entertainment Oxford Hills had to offer, but it was also kind of his home now. That meant that he had every right to benefit from the chaos that engulfed it.

He reluctantly went back inside, through the lounge and back down the sauna hallway. As he passed one of the sauna rooms, a familiar sound caught his ear and Lennie paused briefly to listen to a couple having loud sex.

Well… it still beats beach babysitting; the boy thought to himself. *Plus, I've got a lot to learn.*

CHAPTER 10

MIDNIGHT TRAIN TO LEWISTON

"But who's got time like that to waste
A wise man asked me to my face
If they wrote a book about your life
Would anyone care besides your wife"

(1985)

"Nancy!" Dave said, nudging his wife as the alarm blared. "Nancy…time to wake up!" She groaned and snuggled deeper into the warmth of the blankets. It was the end of August, and the nights were already starting to feel cooler. For Dave's wife, it was always a tradeoff. Colder nights meant more work keeping the fire going, but it also put her husband in the mood for snuggling.

"Come on, Nancy!" her husband urged, sitting up in bed and pulling on his jeans. "Go wake up the little ones, and I'll get Lennie."

Nancy sighed and flicked on the bedside lamp. "David…" she muttered through gritted teeth, slipping out of bed and pulling on the same dress she'd worn earlier that day. "I'm so tired of this crazy shit. Why can't you just find a tenant who actually pays their rent?"

She searched for a jacket, rubbing her bare arms for warmth.

"Because, Nancy," Dave said as he tied his boots, "when there's an opportunity to make a profit with zero overhead, we take it. Even if it means waking up at 11 PM. And since the whole family will benefit, we should all help."

Nancy knew he was right, but the irony of the arrangement still gnawed at her. This was the same man who wouldn't let the kids drink soda—and tonight, they were heading to the J.J. Nissen factory in Lewiston, where a tenant who owed Dave rent worked the night shift. To make up for his debt, the tenant allowed Dave and his family to fill the back of his truck, not just with bread, but with junk food that the factory also distributed locally.

Dave was always open to creative solutions when tenants couldn't pay their rent. It's how the family ended up with a new TV, a four-wheeler, and an eight-week-old puppy named Cherrrychuk. The deal with this tenant was simple: every monthly haul would reduce the outstanding debt by twenty percent.

Dave was keen to maximize their haul. So, he'd built sideboards on the truck to increase its capacity, ensuring they got more than their money's worth. After each trip, he'd sell the goods—mainly to elderly women, at a fraction of grocery store prices—from the sauna.

"We've got to get moving," Dave said. They both left the room to wake the kids.

By 11:30 PM, the whole household was outside in the driveway. Nancy held two squirming toddlers, one on each hip, bouncing them gently as they listened to the nighttime chorus of crickets. After a few minutes, Dave and Lennie finished clearing out the truck cab, and the engine roared to life.

"All set?" Dave said. "Everyone hop in!" Nancy and the kids climbed into the sauna truck. With very little conversation, the truck rumbled down dark back roads and thirty-five minutes later they were approaching the lights of Lewiston. As they got near their destination, Dave broke the silence. "So, everyone knows the drill, right?"

From the back, Walter, who was nearly five years old and surprisingly upbeat for the hour, cheered, "Yup! Get as much as we can and fast!"

"That's right," he grinned. "No slacking off during the heist!" He pulled into the factories parking lot and found an empty space next to an open loading dock.

Walter needed no further prompting. Over the past few months, he'd consumed more junk food than he ever imagined possible. Dave had always enforced a strict no-junk-food rule at home, but the opportunity in Lewiston had been too good to pass up. So, he adjusted his strategy, reasoning that if he allowed the kids to overindulge, they might get it out of their systems.

"Stay here. I'll be right back," Dave ordered before jumping out of the truck, leaving Nancy and the kids in silence. Lennie sat quietly, his mind racing. *What if they got caught?* He knew what they were doing wasn't exactly legal. The younger kids didn't understand, but he sure did. *Would he end up in jail? Or worse, would he be sent back to live with his mom in Massachusetts?* He didn't want that. He loved his mom, but life with her felt so different. Safe, yes—but predictable.

A few minutes later, Dave returned and walked behind the truck. He lowered the tailgate, jumped back into the cab, and slowly backed the truck towards the loading dock before stopping just a few feet away. The tailgate bridged the gap between the vehicle and the dock.

"Okay, let's go! Let's go! Let's go!" he called, and the whole family jumped out of the vehicle, followed him into the building, and began the surreal task of loading up junk food in the middle of the night.

Each child gravitated toward their favorite treat. Lennie grabbed Devil Dogs, Walter hoisted blueberry pies, and little Heidi focused on Twinkies, which her dad had told her were gold bars and worth much more than what her brothers were focused on.

"Hey, Dad?" Lennie called, approaching with a backpack full of cream-filled cakes.

"Yeah?" Dave asked, pausing for a moment.

"Can I take these back with me to Mom's tomorrow?" the boy asked. He was heading back to Massachusetts in the afternoon and imagined it would be nice to have a stash of hidden treats available for the ride down.

"Sure," his dad agreed. His ex-wife could worry about the details.

Twenty minutes later, the truck was packed to the brim with junk food, and the tired crew loaded back into the truck, like pirates returning from a successful raid. As they drove home, and the kids cheerfully helped themselves to some of the booty, Dave wondered if his plan might take a little bit longer than he anticipated.

————

The next morning, Lennie sat at the sauna bar, waiting for his ride to Boston. "Wait, whose bringing me down to Mom's today?" he asked his dad as he emptied his cereal bowl. Although he was now living with his father full-time, once a month he would make the trip down to see his mother for the weekend.

"I already told you," Dave replied. "John's taking you down. He'll drop you off at the Dunkin' Donuts on Route 1 in Saugus." This strategic move would not only save him a six hour round trip, but it would provide an extra level of protection since his buddy would be transporting a large amount of marijuana down as well.

Lennie's confusion melted into recognition. "Oh, that John!" he said with confidence. Many of Dave's sauna patrons had nicknames hoisted upon them—*Big Dick, Little Dick, Crazy Uncle Rick, Johnny the Stripper, Mr. Leisure,* etc.

This time, Lennie's ride down to Massachusetts would be provided by a guy known as *The Hay Thief,* a man who had a reputation for the questionable ways he made money. Rumor had it that John made a steady income stealing hay from Maine farmers and re-selling it at horse farms in Massachusetts. In comparison, transporting a couple pounds of weed, was a piece of cake.

A few minutes later, the bell on the front door jingled, and in walked a large Native American man.

"Hey, John!" Dave called, rising from his chair to greet him.

"What's up, paleface!" John grinned, shaking Dave's hand with his much larger one. "He all set?" he asked towards the young boy.

"Yep!" Lennie said, quickly grabbing his backpack and heading for the door. "See ya, Dad!" He didn't bother hugging his father. After all, he wasn't a kid anymore, and his dad wasn't much of a hugger.

"See you in a few weekends, Lennie!" Dave called, waving. "Thanks, John. Drive safe."

————

As the young boy climbed into John's beat-up 1975 Vega, he was hit with the stale scent of tobacco that lingered in the air; a sharp reminder of countless cigarettes smoked in a very cramped space. There was also the faint, yet unmistakable, aroma of whisky clinging to the upholstery, adding a heavier note to the air. Even the pine-scented air freshener, which was hanging from the rearview mirror, failed to mask all the peculiar odors.

As the mix of smells settled in the back of Lennie's throat, he rolled down the window to let in some fresh air.

"Seat belt?" John asked as he started the engine.

"Dad never makes me," Lennie lied.

The Big Man shrugged. "Okay then."

The ride down was uneventful, punctuated only by the driver's occasional swearing at truckers who came too close for his comfort. Lennie dozed off, waking only when the car stopped roughly two and a half hours later.

"This is your stop kid," John indicated as he pulled into the parking lot of a Dunkin' Donuts. He handed Lennie a five-dollar bill he took from the cupholder. "Your dad said to grab something to eat while you wait for your mom."

"Thanks," Lennie mumbled sleepily, before grabbing his backpack. He stepped out of the car and watched the older man pull away before making his way inside. He sat at a corner table, hoping his mom would arrive soon.

A middle-aged waitress approached. "Hi there, sweetie! I'm Maple. What can I get you?"

The young boy realized how hungry he was. He looked up at the waitress. "Umm... Yeah, I'll have a honey dip donut and chocolate milk."

Maple scribbled down the order. As she turned to leave, she caught sight of a bruise under Lennie's eye. "You okay, honey?" she asked, concerned.

Lennie nodded, his hand instinctively covering the mark. "Yeah. I'm fine," he lied and turned his attention towards the window, which had a full view of the parking lot. He noticed a white Ford Escort resembling his mother's car, pulling into the lot. *Great...* he thought...*She's here and I didn't even get a chance to eat.* But a small balding white-haired man got out of the car and the boy felt a twinge of disappointment.

Maple returned with his order. "Here you go, sweetie!" she said, placing the donut and milk in front of him. "Are you sure you're, ok?"

Lennie was caught off guard. "Yeah...I thought my mom was here, but..." He cut himself off. He was already feeling embarrassed enough. He didn't need anyone probing further.

"No worries sweetie! Just let me know if you need anything else," she reassured him.

Dave's oldest son quickly devoured his meal, letting out a sigh of resignation as he set the milk carton down, and turned his gaze back to the window. *Had his mom forgotten about the pickup?* He wondered if he might have to hitch a ride home. It wasn't like her to be late—not like this.

As he considered his options, Maple appeared at his table and placed another honey glazed donut on the table. "Here you go sweetie!"

"Oh, I don't have any more money," answered Lennie sheepishly.

"This one's on the house," she said, leaving him in peace.

Figuring he might be their longer than anticipated, Lennie repositioned himself so he could view the Star Trek episode playing on a small television that was sitting on the corner counter.

Over the next half-hour the waitress brought him a third donut, a second chocolate milk, and finally a hot chocolate topped with whipped cream. Unbeknown to the boy, she had also placed a phone call to the Saugus Police Department, quietly alerting them to the presence of the young boy with a noticeable bruise on his face, and no apparent guardian.

Nearly a half hour after beginning his unexpected feast, two Saugus cops walked in the coffeeshop and moved in unison over towards where the waitresses were huddling. Maple quietly indicated that it was the boy in the corner table that they were looking for.

Lennie looked up from the television and saw two officers standing in front of him. "I understand you are waiting for your mother?" one of the officers asked. "These ladies say you've been here for quite a while," he paused. "We're going to need to take you into the police station and figure out what's going on. You ever been in a cop car before?" he asked, urgently trying to make it sound like the kind of adventure any young boy would crave.

Lennie was intrigued by the offer. "No, I haven't... but it might not be such a good idea right now — she should be here soon!" he tried to sound convincing.

After a little negotiation and a promise by the waitress to point his mom in the right direction when she arrived, he reluctantly accompanied the officers to their vehicle, and they set off in the direction of the Saugus police station. Upon their arrival they got him a can of soda and ordered him some Chinese food.

Soon, the questions started coming in his direction.

"How long have you been away from your parents?" the captain on duty asked, pulling a chair up next to Lennie. The boy explained his situation, hoping that, with a few more details, things could be sorted out to everyone's liking.

The captain, who was accustomed to family members withholding information during questioning—especially kids trying to protect their parents—waited patiently for Lennie to finish chewing. Once the boy swallowed, he leaned in slightly, his tone shifting to one of gentle concern. "Are you running away from someone? Did someone hit you?"

Lennie paused, the question hanging in the air for a moment as his thoughts swirled. "No," he replied, his voice a bit quieter now. "I told you; I'm waiting for my mother to pick me up."

As for the bruise on his face, he quickly covered for his dad, explaining that it had come from a fistfight with another boy. The truth was, getting the occasional backhand from his father, was an occupational hazard. Dave still believed in some very old-school methods of discipline, and if Lennie was honest with himself, he generally deserved whatever came his way.

"Do you have a phone number we can call?" the captain requested.

To help move things along, the young boy provided a phone number to the sauna. As he chewed on some Crab Rangoon, he heard the desk sergeant loudly questioning the voice on the other end of the line. "Mr. Graiver, we have your son here at the Saugus Police Dept. Would you like him back?"

"Not really," said Dave sarcastically. "He is supposed to be with his mother by now". He felt no compulsion to share the stark reality of the situation; that his son had been sent down to his mothers in a car driven by an ex-con, filled with cannabis, and then casually dropped off alone at a donut shop on Rt. 1, the busiest road in Massachusetts.

Just as the conversation was getting a bit too specific for his taste, Rachel frantically burst into the police station alongside Dave's mother, Queenie. Out of breath, she explained to the desk sergeant that over the last two hours they had made the rounds of just about every Dunkin' Donuts on Route 1. After a half dozen stops, they found the one where her son had been left for pick up.

As they departed the police station, Rachel let out a stream of Yiddish curse words aimed at her ex-husband that even Queenie felt was appropriate. Lennie wondered what the big deal was. He had rather enjoyed the day.

———

After this, the boy started traveling back and forth via the Greyhound bus. It held none of the adventure that came from hitching rides with sauna customers. But apparently it made at least one of his parents feel a bit better about things.

CHAPTER 11

COCAINE'S A WONDERFUL DRUG

"Cocaine's a wonderful drug
Cocaine's a wonderful drug
You may not see what it does for me
But cocaine's a wonderful drug"

(1986)

The last day of 1986 started quietly enough. Dave was up early, splitting wood, while Nancy got busy making French toast for the kids. The sun had barely crept over the horizon, as she moved between the stove and the sink, flipping the thick slices of bread and humming Tanya Tucker's *Delta Dawn* softly to herself.

For the moment, the house felt peaceful. The kids were still asleep upstairs, and she finally had a moment to reflect on the year. Overall, it had been a good one, she reminded herself, despite some growing tension between her and her husband. But their kids were all alive and healthy, and that was enough for now.

After breakfast the family relocated over to the sauna for the afternoon and the day took a more chaotic as the peaceful quiet of the farm was replaced by the roar of cars speeding up Paris Hill. It was a jarring contrast, and it always returned a tightness to Nancy's shoulders.

Sometime around mid-day, Saul's old truck, a clunky beater with rust spots in all the wrong places, pulled into the driveway. The tires skidded over the snow-covered gravel, kicking up a white cloud that billowed behind him like a storm chasing him down.

Saul didn't hesitate. He was already out of the truck and striding toward the sauna building lounge before the engine had even quieted. Inside, Dave looked up from his chair, grinning wide. "Just the guy I was looking for!" he called out, offering his friend a warm welcome. "Come on, let's get to Sauna Six. We've got some catching up to do!"

Nancy arrived just in time to catch the end of the conversation. "David! We're going out tonight, so try and keep the day productive," she encouraged her husband. "Don't you have to get your place ready for the party?" she added, focusing on the new arrival.

Saul caught her eye, his grin fading slightly as he wiped the sweat off his brow with the back of his hand. "It's all about balance, Nancy," he said with a slow nod, like that somehow explained everything.

Nancy rolled her eyes and turned back to the load of laundry she was tackling while her husband and his best friend disappeared down the hallway.

Four hours later, the two men emerged from Sauna Six, eyes red, pupils dilated and flushed faces dripping in sweat. Both were talking a mile a minute and enthusiastically interrupting the other. Saul was leading the charge, with a high-pitched, excited blur to his voice. Dave was a bit more subdued, though fully animated, and with a big grin plastered to his face.

Nancy, arms crossed tightly over her chest, stood waiting in the hallway. She raised an eyebrow as she looked them both over, tapping her foot impatiently on the wooden floor. Her skepticism was as clear to the men as the winter sky.

"We just... we just found the sweet spot. That's all." Saul pleaded with her gently.

Dave chuckled beside him, "Best idea we've had all day."

Nancy eyed them with a look that could've frozen the air around them. "What about that balance, Saul?" she asked skeptically, arching an eyebrow. "Seems like you two are a little... off-balance. I mean, four hours in a sauna…I know you weren't getting each other off…or showering. Are you even hearing yourselves?"

Saul held up his hands, as if to offer a peace treaty. "Nancy, you have to—"

"Yeah, yeah," she interrupted, tapping her foot louder. "I've heard it all before. Last time it was *getting in touch with the earth* and now it's *finding the sweet spot*. I'm waiting for the part where you tell me how this all makes sense."

Dave chuckled, slapping Saul on the back. "She's got a point. Maybe we need to share the love a little more evenly next time."

Nancy raised an eyebrow. "You know what?" she said finally, shaking her head. "I'll never understand you two. But I'll give you this—you sure know how to make an afternoon interesting. What's next, then? A twenty-four-hour retreat?"

Saul smiled as if he was letting her in on a secret and winked. "You just have to trust us on this one."

"Trust you guys?" Nancy asked, her voice dripping with disbelief. "That's rich."

Saul grinned wider. "Trust us. That's the sweet spot."

Nancy gave up on what was clearly a futile conversation and tried a different tack. "You're hosting the party tonight, Saul. Maybe you should go home and get things ready?"

Her gaze flickered over to Dave, who offered her a sheepish smile in return.

"We're fine, Nancy. Just a little too much... of everything," Dave said casually as he ran a hand through his hair trying to smooth away the lingering effects of their afternoon indulgence. His fingers were trembling slightly. "No harm done. We'll pull it together."

Nancy sighed and turned his attention back to the kids, who had wandered into the sauna kitchen. Walter was bouncing around excitedly while Heidi hung back by the table, watching her father.

The little girl hesitated for a moment as her eyes scanned Dave's face. "Is Daddy, okay?"

Nancy gave her a soft and reassuring smile. "He's fine, sweetie. Just getting ready for the party tonight, that's all."

It was all she could do not to lecture her husband about his choices and confront him with the quiet alarm that had been building in her. For a couple of years, she'd been walking a tightrope, balancing the chaos and comfort of family life, and always making sure the foundation was solid on her side. But there were some cracks showing in their relationship, and they were getting more pronounced with each passing day.

"Everything's fine," she repeated, her voice barely a whisper. The words felt hollow, and as the afternoon wore on, she couldn't shake the feeling that something in their life—her life, their life—might be slipping in the wrong direction.

————

By 6 p.m., Dave had returned from the local Chinese restaurant, arms loaded with enough Lo Mein and steak on a stick to feed the entire family. The strong aroma of garlic, soy sauce, and cooked meat filled the sauna, as he carefully set the bags down on the bar.

"Alright, folks, dinners served!" Dave called out, grinning. "If this doesn't make you forget all your worries, I don't know what will."

Nancy raised an eyebrow, giving him a playful side-eye. "You went all out this time, huh?"

He shrugged. There was a mischievous glint in his eyes. "What can I say? You deserve it after the day we've had. I may have accidentally ordered too much. I think we're going to be eating this for days."

They family piled around the table, plates and chopsticks in hand. For a half hour, they gorged themselves on the spread. Between mouthfuls, they all took turns cracking open their fortune cookies.

"Let's see what fate has in store for us tonight," Dave said with a grin, breaking open his cookie. He unfolded the slip of paper and read aloud. '*You will be showered with unexpected wealth.*' He chuckled. "Finally, a little good news around here."

Lennie, who was sitting at the edge of the table with his fortune cookie already broken open, waved his paper around like a trophy. "Mine says, *A 'new adventure awaits you.*' Guess that means my teenage years are going to be a lot of fun!"

"Can't wait!" Nancy said sarcastically. "And then I'll get to do it again in five years."

After a few reminders about bedtimes—she began clearing the table while her husband gathered up supplies for Saul's party.

"You sure you're good to handle things here tonight?"Nancy asked Dave's oldest son, as she cleaned off the faces of the younger kids.

Lennie looked up confidently. "I've got it covered. You can trust me!"

She eyed him for a long moment before giving him a reluctant nod. "Alright, don't stay up too late. And if anyone needs anything, you know where to find us."

Dave slapped his son on the back as he walked past. "You've got this, kid. Just don't let things get too out of hand, alright?"

Lennie gave him a smile. "Go enjoy your night."

————

As the door shut behind them, Lennie felt a mix of pride and nervous energy. After everything that had happened the previous year—two arrests, one in-school suspension— he'd been surprised when his parents had given him the responsibility of holding down the fort. It felt like an opportunity for redemption, a chance to prove he was no longer the reckless kid he once was.

"Who wants ice-cream?" Dave's oldest son asked enthusiastically.

The excited screams from his siblings made their answer obvious and they accepted his terms: full bowls in exchange for an early bedtime. He knew that bribes had worked well in his dad's world and were completely acceptable just as long as no one got hurt in the process.

Once Walter and Heidi were tucked into an old mattress, Lennie set up in one of the sauna rooms and began flipping through his dad's video porn collection, looking for something suitable to watch. He finally landed on one whose cover promised the kind of girl-on-girl action he was fond of. He stuck the tape in the VCR player and got comfortable in his dad's chair.

Before he could get very far, the sound of screeching tires filled the driveway. the boy quickly zipped up his pants and rushed to the door, where he spotted Nancy climbing out of the driver's seat, her face pale and panicked.

"Lennie, get out here!" she screamed. The boy ran over to the vehicle where his father lay in the backseat —nearly naked, drenched in cold sweat, with his jaw clenched, and tightly gripping his left arm.

"Dad, what's wrong?" his voice was trembling.

"I think he's having a heart attack!" Nancy's voice cracked with urgency. She was desperately trying to keep it together.

"Take him to the hospital!" Lennie had never seen his father so vunerable. Panic seemed the only appropriate response.

"Fuck no!" Dave screamed, as he jolted upright, causing Nancy to jump backwards. He had a large amount of cocaine still coursing through his system, and a trip to the ER would mean a lot of explaining. "Call Steve Mason. His number's on the wall!"

His son wasn't sure who Steve Mason was. But he could see his dad was in no condition to provide additional clarity and he rushed inside to make the call.

———

Fifteen minutes later, a bright red Audi screeched into the

driveway, its tires skidding on the snow as the car came to a sliding stop. Out stepped a man wearing aviator sunglasses and a polyester suit left over from the seventies, followed by a woman in a tight black dress, who looked to be utterly bewildered by the turn her New Year's Eve had taken.

"Having the usual good time, Dave?" Steve asked with a lazy grin and a tone laced with almost mocking familiarity. As an emergency room doctor, chaos was second nature to him, and he didn't seem to be particularly phased by the mess in front of him. His eyes scanned his buddy's face which was dripping with sweat from his forehead.

Nancy, tried to suppress the nausea rising in her throat, and shot the doctor a look. "Just get him checked out!" she said through clenched teeth, her voice barely above a whisper. The tight knot of dread in her stomach was growing, and she just wanted answers, to make sure her husband was going to be okay.

Steve didn't seem bothered by her urgency. He took his time walking over to his patient like it was just another typical house call. Dave recoiled at first from any kind of examination, but after some less then gentle prodding from his wife, he finally agreed to let Steve take a closer look at him. More out of guilt than concern—he knew his buddy would rather be tending to the woman in tow.

Steve placed his fingers on Dave's wrist, checking his pulse with practiced indifference. Nancy watched, arms folded tightly across her chest, still reeling from the direction that evening had taken. She could see how pale her husband's face was, but, too her irritation, the doctor didn't seem at all concerned.

After a thorough examination, The doctor straightened up and let out a soft exhale. "Nancy, bring this man two aspirin and a ginger ale," he said calmly, as if he was talking about a patient with a hangover.

Nancy blinked in disbelief. "You can't be serious," she muttered under her breath, as she tried to process the absurdity of the situation. *Two aspirin. Ginger ale. That was the extent of it?* The man she loved—who had just been writhing in pain and sweating through his clothes—was being treated like he had simply had too much to drink.

But fifteen years of cocaine use had taught Steve a few tricks. Within minutes of swallowing the aspirin, Dave was sitting up, and fully coherent. He was still sweating and shaky, but the intense pain had passed and so had the nights urgency.

"Let's head back to my office," he suggested struggling to his feet. There was a slight stagger as he walked, but the worst was clearly over. In sauna six he settled up with his buddy for his emergency visit, bartering some party favors not easily obtained, even by someone with a prescription pad and a DEA number.

"Appreciated!" the doctor said before placing the vial in his pants pocket. He paused and looked his patient in the eye. "Can I suggest you play smarter next time?"

Dave didn't respond. At some point, he was going to need to give the powder a rest, but New Year's Eve didn't feel like the right time to make any drastic decisions. And really, *what did a doctor know anyway?*

Later that night, Lennie lay awake in bed for hours, replaying the scene in his head. His dad had always seemed invincible, almost immortal and the thought that he'd nearly died, rattled through the young boy's mind like a drumbeat. It was a moment that was never supposed to come, and he wondered if the universe was paying him back for putting his brother and sister to bed early, just so he could masturbate.

Nancy had no better luck getting any rest, and she spent the rest of the night watching her husband's chest rise and fall, counting the seconds between each breath. She wasn't entirely confident in the medical judgment of his cokehead friend, and it wasn't until dawn broke that she was finally able to fall asleep.

Dave woke up groggy and sore but determined to make up for lost time. He stumbled down to sauna six, snorted a bump, and justified it to himself, *After all...It's New Year's Day.*

CHAPTER 12

THE DEAD COME TO TOWN

"But you should know that I' just getting started
and your neighbors a pretty good guy
So, forget that old time religion
And give hedonism a try"

(1988)

"Dad!" Lennie shouted, bursting into the farmhouse kitchen, waving a copy of the *Sun-Journal*. "They're coming!"

Dave, who'd been half-heartedly washing the breakfast dishes, turned off the faucet and let the task go. "Slow down, kid. Who's coming?"

His son slapped the paper down on the kitchen table, eyes wide with excitement. "The Dead!" he said, practically bouncing with energy.

Dave wasn't exactly surprised by the news. He'd been hearing rumors for weeks from the local bikers, who'd caught wind of things from their brothers out in California. Then came the whispers from the folks at the racetrack. Even the DJs on Portland radio had been speculating.

And now, here it was, front and center on the newspaper's front page: the Grateful Dead were wrapping up their summer tour on the East Coast with a two-show run at the Oxford Plains Speedway—a ten-minute drive from the sauna—on July 2nd and 3rd.

"They're playing at the Speedway! Dad, we've *got* to go! It's going to be a wild scene!" Lennie insisted with his mind already racing with possibilities. He'd met a ton of hippies at the sauna over the years, and the women—always kind and never bothered by a curious young boy—had left a lasting impression. The idea of being surrounded by thousands of them felt almost too good to be true.

Dave glanced at the paper, then back at his son, mulling it over. Personally, he could take or leave the Dead's music. He'd seen them play a few times back in the '70s—Portland, Bangor, Augusta—and they were always a fun show. But his tastes leaned more toward what people were now calling classic rock. He'd have been far more excited if the Eagles were coming through.

But there was no denying the Dead's cultural impact. In the past few years, they'd exploded in popularity after one of their songs, *Touch of Grey* cracked the top forty. What was once a band known for songs that stretched into thirty-minute cosmic journeys had managed to condense their essence into a tight four-minute, fifty-three-second radio hit.

And then the video—a wildly creative, animated sequence by a director from *Sesame Street*—had turned the band members into skeletons, which played non-stop on MTV. As a result, the Dead's crowds were growing bigger by the day.

Dave looked at his son's eager face and tried to share in his excitement. "I suppose this could be a good opportunity…" he began, his mind already turning the idea over. "Okay, we'll go," he said, a plan quickly coming together. There just might be a way to make it work for all parties involved.

"Yes!" Lennie cheered, pumping his fist in the air.

"But…" Dave continued, the gears turning in his head. "…you're going to have to help me."

His son hesitated. "Help you with what, Dad?" he asked, cautiously. The last thing he wanted was for anything to get in the way of him chasing after hippie girls in colorful dresses.

"First —" Dave said, scribbling something on the edge of the paper, "we'll need to make a beer run. Believe it or not, hippies love beer. But they're *not* going to pay five dollars a cup at the Speedway!"

He was already lost in thought.

"Oh," Lennie said, starting to understand. "You want to work the show?" he guessed, masking his disappointment.

"And there are a few other things we'll need to stock up on," his dad continued, ignoring his son's question as he jotted down notes. "Deadheads love their weed. Maybe even more than their music."

"True," the boy agreed, quite familiar with the like a skunk like smell in the sauna rooms after the longhairs left.

"But finding anything locally grown is a bust right now, so we'll have to head to the city and see who's got some of that Mexican brick weed." Dave added it to his list.

"Anything else?" Lennie was starting to get the sense that he and his father had very different priorities, but he didn't want to put a stop to the trip. Not with the circus about to roll into town.

Dave smiled at his son's silent approval and mentally added cocaine to the list. "Looks like we've got our work cut out for us, son!" he said, clapping him on the back. "Help me plan this right, and we're not just going to make a ton of cash—you might even get laid! Those hippie girls are always open to *possibilities*!"

Lennie felt a rush of heat to his face. He wasn't quite ready to acknowledge the surge of hormones coursing through him, at least not to his dad. But the mess of crusty socks by his bed —made it as clear as day.

The next month passed quickly, and before long it was early Saturday morning on the day of the first show. After an early breakfast, Lennie helped load up the back of his dad's truck with cases of warm beer and at least one container full of *dime* bags."

When everything was loaded up, he closed the tailgate, just as his dad arrived with a large blue tarp.

"Okay, that's everything!" Dave said with a satisfied grin, tossing the tarp over one side of the truck bed. "Tie it up!"

Lennie walked around to the other side. "I don't think I'll ever understand how you became such a morning person, Dad," he remarked as he secured the tarp.

"Trust me, son…" his father said, climbing into the driver's seat. "…if we don't get there early and set up, we might as well not even go. It's all about location!"

Lennie sighed and took his place in the passenger seat. They made a quick stop in town to pick up a couple of his friends, and then headed for the Speedway, taking all the backroads they knew. Even with the shortcuts, the ride still took almost an hour, and it became clear that some local had spilled the beans about the back ways into the racetrack.

But the sun was shining, and Lennie wasn't bothered by the delay. He kept his hand out the window the entire ride, and remained lost in the important question of just how many topless girls he might see. The other passengers kept quiet, and the short journey took on the mood of a religious pilgrimage.

———

Just as dad predicted, things were already in full swing at the Speedway when they arrived. They found a good parking spot near a row of porta-potties with a perfect view of where the band would play that evening and wasted no time setting up their makeshift operation.

By 11 a.m., the crowd had grown to over 100,000, and traffic had backed up twenty miles, all the way to Gray. The five Oxford County Sheriff's deputies had long since given up on crowd control and were now huddled in the shade across the street, assessing the chaos from a safe distance.

Around noon, Dave spotted his buddy wading through the throng and waved him over. "Hey, Saul!"

"Dave! Lennie!" Saul said, making his way toward them. "What's going on here?" he asked, grinning knowingly. The young boy ignored the question, preoccupied with customers seeking party favors and his dad answered for the two of them.

"What—*this*?" Dave said sarcastically. "You really think we'd miss out on an opportunity like this?"

His buddy chuckled. "I'm just jealous. It took me forever to get in here. All up and down Rt. 26 people are renting out their lawns for parking and camping and charging a buck to use their bathrooms. I saw at least half a dozen lemonade stands and people grilling burgers and dogs on their front lawns. It's like the Fryeburg Fair out there!"

Dave laughed. "Shakedown Street has arrived in Oxford Hills. Nice change for the locals, huh?"

"Yup. Depending on your perspective, it's either a banquet for the senses or a full-on assault," Saul added, noticing an older Speedway employee scowling as he tried to navigate through a crowd filled with bare chested hippies playing guitar, hacky sack circles and girls in sundresses.

Dave inhaled deeply, the air rich with a combination of weed, patchouli, pheromones, gasoline, propane, dust, and grilled meat. "Unfortunately, the intoxicating mix was quickly overwhelmed when the breeze shifted and the unmistakable stench from the nearby toilets him them full force.

Meanwhile, Lennie stayed busy hustling beer from the back of the truck. During a brief lull, one of the girls from the hacky sack circle came over to check out their set-up. She wore a crown of dandelions and looked about his age.

"So…" she said with a playful grin, "…what do you have that I can smoke?"

Lennie pulled out a baggie from their stash.

"That's it?" she asked, raising an eyebrow after inspecting it. "I expected better from Maine."

"Oh, this isn't from Maine," Lennie said a little too quickly.

She crossed her arms and gave him a teasing look, "So, there's no good weed left in Maine?"

The boy shifted uncomfortably. "Maybe… there might be some out there. But mostly all the good stuff's gone for the season. At least until October."

She leaned in closer, and whispered, "Tell you what. I'll go find the good stuff…and then you come find me later."

Before he could respond, she had already turned and disappeared into the crowd.

———

The rest of the afternoon dragged for Lennie who spent most of it scanning the lot, hoping for another glimpse of his new friend. By late afternoon, the truck was out of inventory, and ticket holders began heading inside the Speedway. The scene outside grew sketchier with ticketless hippies wandering the lot, requesting a *miracle*, shady underworld commerce facilitated with the whispers of *nugs*, or *boomers* and with the only consistent sound being the hiss of balloons as they got filled by semi-clandestine nitrous tanks.

Dave took it all in with a satisfied grin. The only thing he could criticize was his peers' complete lack of subtlety or style.

"Hey, Dad, since we're done here, I'm going to check things out, okay?" Lennie interrupted.

Dave knew his son wasn't really asking for permission. "Okay, but be back before dusk. There are going to be a lot of hippies looking for a place to clean up later tonight."

Lennie gave him a half-hearted nod before disappearing into the crowd. He hoped to find the girl he'd spoken to earlier—or at the very least, someone like her.

CHAPTER 13
I SWEAR HE'S MY NEPHEW

"I swear he's my nephew
You know I wouldn't lie
Or maybe a distant cousin
Someone on my father's side"

(1989)

By late March, and after the onslaught of winter, cabin fever was rampant throughout western Maine. With the days getting longer, the extended sunlight was encouraging many of the sleeping grizzly Mainers out of hibernation and back into civilization. It could be a strangely challenging thing, to break simple winter habits of eat, sleep, survive and repeat.

Dave was sitting in his chair, only half following a few regulars playing pool, when he noticed a Volkswagen Jetta pull up on the gravel outside. A man who looked to be in his early fifties stepped cautiously out of the driver's seat, grabbed a gym bag from the backseat, and made his way toward the sauna entrance. Behind him, a younger man in his twenties, casually stylish and slightly built, emerged from the passenger side, and followed.

Inside the sauna, they were greeted by the inviting aroma of garlic, tomato sauce, and freshly baked bread. Nancy stood behind the bar, her hands moving in a steady, hypnotic rhythm as she kneaded a large ball of pizza dough. The only interruption to her flow was the occasional glance at the oven timer to keep track of the time.

"Frank!" Dave greeted the new arrivals with his usual welcoming tone. Frank was a confirmed bachelor and the general manager at a car dealership on Main St. in South Paris. He was a regular visitor to the sauna, sometimes solo, but occasionally in the company of younger men.

"Hey Frank!" piped in Nancy from behind the bar. "How are you doing?

Nancy had always liked Frank, who was also well-kept, a rare find at the bottom of Paris Hill. He was quiet, kind and one of the few men she could sit and have a conversation with that wouldn't leave her husband feeling jealous. The younger man, however, was a stranger to the sauna regulars, sparking immediate curiosity— although no one showed it outright.

Nancy always felt a little sad for Frank and his perpetual bachelor status, and she would often try pairing him up with one of the single women hanging around the sauna. She saw it as a win-win. Frank wouldn't be alone, and there would be one less woman in the dating pool in these parts, which, to her, sometimes felt like a bottomless bucket.

"Oh, you know…" Frank reached up to scratch the back of his head. "…just busy with work. Plus, it's been too cold to even think about going out," he added matter-of-factly.

Well, the good news…" said Dave, rising from his chair, "… is that the sauna's are running hot tonight, so you will have no problem shaking off the chill. He turned his attention to Franks companion. "Who's your friend?

The older man paused for a moment, and his cheeks grew flushed. "This is —"

The younger man cut him off. "Hi, I'm Gary" he said extending his hand to Dave's. "I'm just up visiting my uncle Frankie for the weekend"

"Frank!" said Nancy wiping her hands clean on her apron and stepping out from behind the bar. "You never told us you had a nephew. And a young and handsome one at that!" she finished with one hand on each of Gary's shoulders as she approvingly looked him over.

"Yeah..." Frank confirmed reflexively. "He's my brother's son... from away!"

"Really?" Nancy was intrigued. "Where are you from Gary?

"Well," said the younger man, clasping her hand in his. "Originally, I'm from Washington, but I'm going to school now down in Portland. I'm working on my bachelor's in fine arts."

Nancy turned to look at Frank, "What a delightful family you have Frank, you should be proud."

The older man smiled nervously. "Hey, did I hear you say you had a sauna ready for us Dave?" He was anxious to wrap up the conversation.

"That I did!" said Dave with a look of amusement on his face. "Sauna four is ready when you are. You guys need towels or something to drink?"

"We're all set. We brought our own wine," Gary said opening his shoulder bag and revealing a bottle of White Zinfandel and two wine glasses.

"A couple of towels would be great!" Frank quickly added.

Nancy smiled and handed them each a towel before they headed down the hall.

"Alright... well... enjoy!" she encouraged.

———

As the door closed behind them in the changing room, Frank spun Gary around, forcibly pressed him up against the wall and began grinding up against his crotch. He always found Dave's welcoming hazing strangely arousing, and his partners usually benefitted as a result.

"Slow down *Uncle* Frank!" Gary laughed and pulled away from the older man.

Both men quickly got undressed and headed into the warmth of the sauna. Frank looked on hungrily as the younger man got covered in steam. He felt a little creepy taking his date to the sauna on their first outing, but Oxford Hills had limited options for gay friendly get-togethers, and Dave's had some obvious advantages.

Gary, on the other hand, seemed unfazed by the secrecy of it all. He had been to more than a few places like this before. But there was something about the small-town sauna that felt different, more intimate and more insistent. And wonderfully naughty. He made a mental note to continue dating men from outside of Portland.

Before the heat could shut him down, Frank pulled his date close and let the soft brush of his lips come up against his date's ear. In response, Gary grasped the older man's rigid cock, and Frank let out a low moan.

"Quite the family reunion wouldn't you say?" he asked with a mischievous smile.

———

"Well, that was… something," Gary lingered in the doorway, looking the lounge over. He kicked off his flip-flops and pulled up a stool at the bar.

"First time?" Nancy asked curiously.

"Yeah," Gary said, his lips twitching into a half-smile. "Uncle Frank convinced me to give it a try. Says it's good for the muscles, you know?"

"You should've told me you were bringing a rookie," Dave chimed in as Frank also returned out to the lounge area. "I would've given you the full tour." He gestured with an exaggerated flourish to the lounge area.

"Next time, maybe," Frank said with a shrug, anxious to move towards a nightcap at his apartment. Gary, however, seemed to be just getting started.

"It was intense…the heat" Gary admitted, running a hand through his wet hair. "Right Uncle Frank?"

Frank nodded uncomfortably.

"Yep, it's a good reset!" Nancy added confidently.

"Yeah, like an enema for the soul," Gary remarked dryly.

Frank stood up, slinging his gym bag over his shoulder. "Well, it's about that time," he said.

His date took the hint and stood up. "Yeah, I guess so."

Frank turned and allowed a faint smile to cross his lips. "Thanks for the sauna, Dave."

"Bye handsome!" Gary waved in Dave's direction as he departed.

Once the door had closed behind them, Nancy eyes drifted to Dave.

"I always thought Frank's brother had a daughter?" she asked.

Dave smiled, grateful for her naivete. It usually worked in his favor.

CHAPTER 14

MO' BARRELS OF MONEY

**"They got their homes they got their banks
And stocks and bonds to fill their tanks
I do my banking in my shorts
And bury barrels in the woods"**

(1990)

With the mail in one hand and the butt end of a joint in the other, Dave turned the knob on the front door of the sauna, setting off its familiar jingle. A breeze carrying the scent of autumn leaves followed him inside, mingling with the comforting smells of burning wood and freshly laundered towels. It was a quiet afternoon—Nancy had taken the kids to a doctor's appointment, leaving Dave with a few hours to himself. Or, almost to himself.

"Anything good?" asked a freshly showered woman who was standing in front of the fireplace and puffing on her own joint. She smiled at him before tossing the roach and taking a seat in his recliner.

"Doubt it," he replied as he began sifting through the pile of mail. There was the usual junk—solicitations from foresters hoping to log his land, a Cinemax subscription offer, the monthly water bill—and then a government-issued envelope that caught his eye. Dave hesitated. "Fuck…"

"What is it?" the woman asked as she got up and walked over to the bar where he was reading the letter.

"It's from the IRS…" Dave said, his voice trailing off as he paused.

By now, the woman was leaning over Dave's back, trying to get a better look at the letter.

"Josephine, give me some space, will you?" he muttered trying to read the letter for the second time. *And why are you still here? he thought to himself.*

The letter was clear. The IRS had noticed some of Dave's recent purchases over the past year—things like a house on Lake Thompson in Oxford, a two-family unit on Key Summerland in Florida, and a new wood processor. They'd also done the math, and the numbers didn't match up with the income he and Nancy had reported. The letter indicated that in a couple of weeks, they'd be knocking on his door, with questions.

"Fuck!" he said, repeating his earlier exclamation. "What do these bastards want with me?"

"Ouch, Dave… you're being audited?" Josephine asked, her voice tinged with curiosity. She pulled back from his chair and started packing up her sauna toiletries.

Dave looked up from the letter, his gaze shifting to her. "Did Jim do this?" he asked, anger creeping into his voice.

Josephine avoided his eyes, running a hand through her tight, curly copper hair, before answering. "How the hell would I know? You've got plenty of enemies. Why jump to conclusions?

"From my experience, most men don't take too kindly to other men fucking their wives," Dave shot back, his eyes narrowing. Lately, he had been getting a string of not-so-veiled threats from her husband.

Josephine rolled her eyes as she slipped into her jean jacket. "I already told you; he thinks it's over between us. As far as he knows, I'm out having a lunch date with my sister right now."

She stood by the door, one hand resting on her hip, the other clutching her bag. *Why does she have to be so damn hot? he thought.* Everything about her was smooth, graceful, and deliberate—as if she was performing a dance. And to make it worse, she had a body that was perfectly proportioned for touch—curves in all the right places—her hair, wild and untamed, and always smelling like lavender soap.

This certainly wasn't the first time Dave had gotten involved with a married woman. Most of the affairs been short-lived and usually without complications. A few angry words exchanged at the local Shop 'n Save, maybe a verbal threat shouted from a truck passing by the sauna—was usually the extent of it.

But now, the IRS was involved, and his gut told him that his fling with Josephine might have something to do with it.

"You know what —" Josephine began, but she stopped herself mid-sentence, throwing her bag over her shoulder. "Never mind… I'll see you around, Dave." With that, she made a swift exit, without giving him a chance to respond.

"Damn it!" Dave muttered, crumpling a piece of the junk mail and tossing it into the fire.

————

Later that evening, after the kids were in bed, Dave sat silently at the kitchen table as his wife read the letter. "Well, there are a few things that could work in our favor. None of those properties have paperwork showing the real purchase price, so that might help close some of the income gaps. At least on paper."

Dave crossed his arms and said nothing.

Nancy continued, "We could also claim we used our savings to cover the purchases." But they kept almost no money in the bank, and with only a sketchy paper trail on a declared income of $27,000 he worried that this route would mean admitting to stashing cash in places meant to avoid detection. It wasn't illegal to bury money in barrels, but it would complicate the conversation and was likely to come back to haunt him in any future legal troubles.

Dave sighed, feeling the weight of the situation. He knew he was looking at very few options that made any real sense.

His wife moved closer to him. It wasn't often that she would find her husband reeling from bad news and it surprised her how turned on she was by this kind of energy. "Lucky for you…" her voice softening with a touch of seduction, "…bureaucracies move slowly. The letter says we have three weeks to figure this out." She held out her hand, "For now, why don't you come upstairs with me?"

With little hesitation, Dave allowed her to take him upstairs where she successfully distracted him for the rest of the evening.

———

Twenty-one days later, as if on cue, a black sedan with government plates pulled into the sauna parking lot. As Dave watched from the front window, a sinking feeling began creeping into his stomach.

Nervously, he began folding a pile of towels that were sitting on the pool table, even as his eyes kept flicking back to car. In his mind, he imagined an intimidating IRS agent inside, ready to spring a trap on an unsuspecting civilian.

But when the door of the car opened a few minutes later, it was a short, balding man in his late forties, wearing a drab grey suit that stepped out. His stiff, methodical walk exuded the kind of professionalism that screamed *lifetime desk job*, and for a moment, Dave felt a little less anxious about the encounter.

But the truth was, that despite the twenty-one-day head start, he still didn't have a clear plan for how to handle this situation. With the agent pre-occupied casually appraising the property, Dave had a moment to gather himself and wipe the worry from his face. Just in time for the door to swing open.

"Mr. Graiver?" The agent's voice was monotone, reminding the sauna owner of Sgt. Joe Friday from *Dragnet*.

Dave looked up from the pile of towels. "That's me."

"I'm Special Agent Morriss from the Internal Revenue Service," the man indicated before pausing. "I'm here to discuss some discrepancies we discovered in your most recent tax filings. I'm hoping you can offer an explanation during my visit," the agent said calmly. "Is there a place where I can set up?"

Special Agent, my ass, Dave thought to himself as he continued folding towels, while mentally running through a list of sarcastic one-liners, including: *What's yout superpower? Lethal boredom?*

"Oh yeah. I think I got a letter about something like that," Dave said as casually as possible. "Well, as you can see, I'm pretty busy with work today!" The excuse was weak, considering he had nothing more than a small pile of towels in front of him.

Agent Morriss scanned the empty room and then looked back at Dave with skepticism, unimpressed with his response.

Dave glanced at the clock on the wall. "I guess if you don't mind me moving around a bit, we can talk. Why don't you grab a stool over there? I just need a minute to get fires started in the sauna stoves."

Morriss seemed to be in no hurry, and he grabbed a stool from the bar before making himself comfortable at the pool table. After setting down a folder of papers beside the folded towels, he waited patiently. After a couple of minutes, Dave returned and took a seat across from him.

"So, Mr. Graiver…" the agent paused to look over his paperwork. "…on last year's joint tax filing with your wife, you listed income from six rental properties, firewood sales, and sauna customers. Can you confirm these are your only sources of income, and that the revenue totals are accurate?" He slid a copy of Dave's 1040 form across the table for him to review.

As he pretended to study the form, Dave considered his response. Most of his business was done and off the books, so bank records wouldn't reveal much. But he would be in deep trouble if the agent had somehow traced his unreported real estate acquisitions. For now, playing dumb seemed like his best bet.

"It looks pretty accurate to me," Dave said cautiously, pushing the papers back toward the agent.

Morriss didn't react. "Alright then," he said, with no visible emotion, "Let's keep going."

For the next hour, Dave was bombarded with questions—everything from his accounting practices to the kind of soap he provided to sauna customers. As the afternoon dragged on, it became clear that the agent wasn't interested in wrapping up the conversation any time soon. Instead, he seemed increasingly fascinated by the unique business methodology Dave operated under.

By the time the IRS agent was wrapping up, Dave had folded every towel twice, cleaned the dishes, and even swept the floor spotless. *If I end up in jail,* he thought, *at least Nancy will be happy I left the place in good shape.*

"Well, I think we've covered enough for today," Agent Morriss finally concluded, before making one last note and tucking his papers into his briefcase.

Dave was relieved. "Sounds good. I hope this has been helpful!" he lied.

"We'll see," the agent replied. "You should be hearing from us in about a month." With that, he departed out the front door.

Dave headed back to check on the sauna rooms. "Come on, really?" he muttered to no one as he opened one of the sauna room doors. He had been talking with the agent for so long that the fire had burned out.

Thankfully, the small, dimly lit room was still warm enough for him to stretch out on the top bench. He quickly conjured up memories of a particularly attractive sauna visitor and only minutes later, the last traces of tension from the earlier meeting had been drained away.

Agent Morriss had kept his word, and just over a month after their meeting, Dave found himself heading to the regional IRS office in Portland for a follow-up. Over the previous weeks, the gravity of his situation had slowly sunk in as he realized that he still had no workable plan for escaping the governments grasp. As a result, it had been one long blur of restless nights and endless anxious thoughts.

After parking his vehicle, he warily made his way over to the building entrance. As he stepped into the dimly lit, sterile government building, he was greeted by the familiar scent of copy paper, ink, and old filing cabinets. It brought him back to his days as a teacher in Massachusetts—and those long afternoons spent grading papers in a building that smelled just like the one he was currently in.

He glanced down at the letter in his hand, checked the room number, and then made his way up a flight of stairs. The hallway stretched out before him, lined with more doors and numbered plaques, and he headed deeper into what he assumed was the belly of some bureaucratic beast.

When he reached the end of the hall, he found himself in a large open area with a secretary's desk placed strategically between visitors and a group of offices towards the back.

"Can I help you?" an older women asked sternly as he got closer to the desk.

"I have an appointment with. —" he glanced at the paper in his hand for a name before he was interrupted.

"Mr. Graiver! Hello... I'm Helen Destafano, tax compliance officer here at the IRS."

Dave was startled as an attractive young woman approached him with a warm, welcoming smile. As she extended her hand, Dave noticed her bright blue eyes, long brown hair—and a figure that, even her pantsuit couldn't hide. His eyes flicked down to her hand. No wedding ring. Things were looking up.

"Nice to meet you, Ms. Destafano," Dave replied returning her smile and shaking her hand.

She gestured for him to come inside. "Please, come in and we can get started!"

As Dave willingly followed her into the office, he conceded that perhaps he wasn't entirely doomed. If he was going to be interrogated, it might as well be by someone as appealing as her.

"Thank you for coming in today!" she said gesturing toward a chair in front of her desk.

"My pleasure!" Dave tried to mask the mix of nervousness and arousal that was bubbling inside him. Money laundering, he could handle. Beautiful women…maybe. With her added allure potentially clouding his judgement, he knew he would need to stay sharp.

"So, I've reviewed the information that the field agent provided. If possible, I'd like to clarify some points and then try and fill in some gaps," she offered hopefully.

"Ok," Dave replied, cautiously, knowing the was stepping into uncharted territory.

"Good!" she said cheerfully. "As mentioned in our follow-up letter, and based on your previous interview, we still have some questions about the joint return you and your wife filed last year."

As she continued outlining the issues at hand, Dave tuned her out and attempted to focus on his potential answers. He kept reminding himself that this would be just like closing any deal. Find out what they need to be satisfied and give up nothing beyond that.

"Mr. Graiver, on paper, it looks like you got some extremely good deals on property." The compliance officer sounded almost impressed. "Can you explain this a little bit more?"

Dave shrugged. "I think people just like me!" There was some truth to his statement, and he certainly wasn't going to admit to any part of his real estate deals being done off the books.

Ms. Destafano looked up from her papers, meeting his confident smile with one of her own. "I'll mark that down as *client provided no additional information*," she said with a half-smile. "Now, let's talk about the cash you bring in from your sauna business. Do I understand that these handwritten accounts are your only records? No ledger? No bookkeeper?"

Before Dave could respond, there was a knock at the door. The secretary from out front poked her head into the office. "I'm sorry to interrupt, but can I borrow you for a minute? I'm trying to figure out something on the computer, and I'm not having much luck," she admitted.

"Off course Shelley. I'll be right out!" the supervisor reassured her and turned back to Dave. "Mr. Gravier, I apologize, but I'm going to need a few minutes. But I promise I will be right back?" and with that she stood up and walked out of the office, closing the door behind her.

As Dave sat silently, he scanned the office. On one wall, there was a landscape painting depicting a perfect New England summer day, and a photo of what looked like the family Golden Retriever. On her desk, he spotted the paperwork he'd submitted to the field agent, now scattered like bait.

Sensing a course of action, Dave jumped up and grabbed every third piece of paper from the desk before stuffing them into the back of his pants. Just as he returned to his seat, the door opened, and Ms. Destafano returned.

"I'm so sorry, Mr. Graiver!" she apologized moving back behind her desk, giving no indication that she noticed papers were missing. She quickly returned to her line of questioning.

"So…no bookkeeper then?" she asked.

"Nope, sorry," Dave answered, trying to seem nonchalant.

"Alright, let's talk about your wife's income for the year," she continued, referring to her notes. "Was she a stay-at-home mom the entire time?"

Dave nodded, still trying to anticipate where her line of questioning might lead.

"What about side jobs or outside income?" the supervisor asked, scanning her notes.

As he considered the question, an idea hit him and he realized that he now had a way out. But it would mean throwing Nancy under the bus.

"Oh shit... yeah," Dave said, pretending to recall something. "I totally forgot about her Avon business. She did make a few sales last year." He feigned casual indifference, hoping it sounded convincing.

"Do you have any idea how much income she made from those sales?" Ms. Destafano inquired.

"Not exactly, but I'd guess around $10,000," Dave clarified. "I always forget she's doing it because it's always at someone else's house. For some reason, she never invites me." He hoped his delivery was on point.

After making a note, the tax officer said, "Well, that should help explain some of the discrepancies. Let's talk about any expenses she may have incurred."

After another ten minutes or so, Ms. Destafano's put her pen down on her desk. "Let's call it a day for now. I'll still need those business records from your wife. Once I have those, we should be able to wrap up this audit."

She stood and walked around her desk, offering her hand. "Thank you for making the trip down!"

"Well, you know where to find me if you have any follow up questions," Dave said suggestively. "Either way you should come by the sauna sometime. I'm sure your work can bring on a whole lot of tension." He kept his tone light and clinical, hoping it didn't sound creepy.

"I appreciate the offer, Mr. Graiver," she said, choosing her words carefully. "Maybe I'll take you up on it sometime. Let's see how your case turns out first."

On the drive home, Dave felt just like the boy who had just been promised a cookie from the cookie jar.

A few months later, a letter arrived at the sauna addressed to Nancy from the IRS. With no one around to stop him, Dave sank into his chair and carefully opened it.

It read: *"Dear Mrs. Graiver - The Internal Revenue Service has determined that you failed to report income of approximately $10,000 in 1987 to the Federal Government. This is a Class 3 violation of US Statute and subject to a jail term of up to 3 years in Federal Prison and/or a fine of no less than $500 for each assigned violation. However, the Internal Revenue Service has concluded that, as you did not prepare your own tax return, and may not have been aware of the oversight, you will only be subject to an administrative fine of $360 for failing to report your business income to the government. Please, be advised, however, that your signature on a tax return constitutes your confirmation of its veracity, and any future failure to report all taxable income may be met with harsher penalties."*

Dave put the letter down, exhaling in relief. Leaning back in his chair, he imagined his wife's reaction when he told her she owed the feds $360.

MO' BARRELS OF MONEY

MASSHOLE IN ME

"So once a month I make the trip
to pick up fuel for all thing's hip
my customers demand from me
the stuff that makes their noses bleed"

(1993)

"Hey David, who's the jackass taking up two spots in the parking lot?" Nancy asked curiously as she watched a car with out-of-state plates settle in on the gravel outside.

But Dave wasn't paying much attention to his wife, thanks mostly to the presence of Josephine, whose obvious interest in Nancy's husband was starting to worry her. She was beginning to suspect that there was more going on than either would admit to.

Regardless, it was a moot point as Dave generally took no interest in trying to coordinate where his customers parked. This was true whether the vehicle was in the lot out front or even on one of the adjacent properties.

A few minutes later a man wearing sunglasses, Bermuda shorts, and a porn star moustache paused as he entered, as if expecting a round of applause from the sauna guests. "Man… that parking lot is not easy to navigate!" he said with an accent that clearly placed his roots somewhere in the close vicinity of Fenway Park.

His arrival was met with a collective groan from the crowd gathered around the pool table, which included Saul, a local woodsman named Veiko, and a handful of local waitresses, who were all quite familiar with the energy and the purpose of the visitor from Massachusetts. They also knew that his birth name was Vinnie, although long ago he had been dubbed *Masshole* by sauna regulars. The only person who was genuinely excited by the new arrival was Weird Rob, as it meant he was no longer low man on the totem pole.

Having just provided a personal escort into the changing room for Josephine, Dave emerged from the back hallway. "Leave Vinnie alone!" he said coming to the defense of the recent arrival. "He's from Massachusetts. "He doesn't know any better," he offered as an excuse. "The truth is that I can't afford to paint lines out there," he told the crowd, almost believing it himself.

"You are so fucking cheap!" Nancy said loud enough for anyone to hear, flashing on a decade old memory of Dave making her pay for her share of meals on some family vacation they had once taken. All from the limited take home pay she brought in from waitressing at the time.

"Hey! I bought you breakfast this morning," Dave countered with a mischievous grin, and he geared up to defend himself in what was turning into a very public event.

"Yeah, you cheapskate. Once again you took us to all you can eat buffet over at the Country Way Restaurant. Aren't you the romantic big spender! I'm still surprised they ever let you back in after the incident with Lennie. You remember that fiasco, don't you?" Nancy blurted the words out quicker and with more resentment than she had originally intended. There had never been much romance in Dave's approach to marriage, and dining out locally was generally as far as he had been willing to go to impress his wife.

By now though, he knew that he wasn't doing himself any favors by continuing the dialogue. So, he concluded triumphantly with a simple statement of fact. "Could have been worse. I could have made you pay!"

———

"So how's business?" Dave asked Vinnie as he pulled him

aside, making a rare exception to his rule that if you wanted to talk business, you needed to get their before 5pm.

"Business is good! They like what I'm bringing them and there is nothing like a war on drugs to fuel demand!" the Vinnie said confidently to Dave, stating a basic truth that all successful drug dealers counted on for their success.

"Yup. Thank God for stupid government," Dave agreed. "I plan on feeding my family on ignorance for a long time!"

The Masshole nodded his head before adding, "You want stupid government? Come back to Massachusetts. If you're Irish, you and your drinking buddies can run a city…" he hesitated, "… or at the very least, the police department!" he finished up with a chuckle.

"Sometimes I think about what it would have been like if I stayed in the city," Dave mused out loud. "Not a lot of my tribe here in Oxford Hills." Looking away, he pondered just a little too long, providing his out of state visitor with an opening that other sauna guests only dreamed about, and he started inching towards the chair.

"Don't lose any sleep over it. Too many people…too many cars…too many assholes with college degrees. You were smart to get out when you did!" Vinnie concluded with certainty, settling into the sauna owner's throne like he owned the place.

Dave turned his attention back toward Vinnie. *Masshole…*he thought to himself, pretending not to notice his visitor's indiscretion. After all, the guy was a monthly visitor who made him a lot of money, and that meant cutting him some slack. "I'll get a sauna ready for you… and I'll have a package ready on your way out," he said discreetly.

"Thanks. I'll stay busy out here in the meantime," Vince said smiling, registering the presence of at least a couple of single ladies in the room that might occupy his time.

Western Maine was his kind of place. More than a decade after it ended, the area still felt like it was stuck in a time loop from the seventies, with Aerosmith and Lynyrd Skynyrd providing the everyday soundtrack. Vinnie could see that a moustache like his still had a place in this part of the world, and every time he visited, he felt more and more like he was coming home. Sure, the crew at the sauna made fun of him, but it was the price you paid for being accepted.

————

A few hours later Vinnie emerged from the hallway leading to the sauna rooms and re-entered the lounge area. By now it was empty except for the boss, who was reclined in his chair with his eyes closed. Before he could get too close, a very much awake Dave, half threw him a duffel bag, which ended his approach.

"You know, Dave…" Vinnie began, "…I've been thinking some about relocating up north here. Massachusetts just seems a bit crowded. What do you think?" For a moment, his usual bravado was gone, replaced by an earnest yearning for a life far removed from the one he was currently living.

Dave considered Vinnie's question for a minute before replying. "I think if having to keep a fire going for eight months out of the year sounds romantic…then this is definitely where you wanna be!" Dave had seen more than his share of underprepared newcomers fail over the years, and he struggled to come up with anything as diplomatic as this simple reality check.

Vinnie nodded his head. "I'll keep that in mind. And I will see you in a month, my friend!" he shouted striding out the door. Walking towards his car, he realized that he no longer enjoyed just how much his vehicle stood out in Maine.

From the comfort of his chair, Dave watched the car pull out. *Yeah, he ain't gonna hack it up here*, Dave thought to himself before reconsidering. *Then again… maybe he'll grow into it.*

As for Dave, he was over twenty years in, and western Maine

still suited him just fine. He hadn't just adapted; he had thrived like a feral coyote. But he remembered where he came from and he knew that with a little hard work, and a willingness to bend the rules, other folks from away could also do just fine.

————

"Is it everything you expected when you first moved up here?" Nancy asked, gesturing vaguely to the empty room. "The crowd, the business… all of it."

Dave's eyes flickered to the window, where the sky had darkened, and the last traces of moonlight were fading away. He took a measured sip of his beer before he answered. "No. I never expected it to be quite like this," he admitted.

Nancy raised an eyebrow, a wisp of amusement forming at the corners of her lips. "You are quite good playing the part!"

Dave sat up a little straighter, his eyes meeting hers with a quiet resilience. "I'm not sure I'm faking any of it," he admitted.

Nancy snorted softly, but there was no malice in her voice. "You built something nice here. And Massachusetts has plenty of Jewish guys left to fill your void!"

"Yeah," Dave agreed quietly. "You're probably right."

His wife's expression softened, but there was something else there—something that had been building for a while. She walked over and took a seat next to him, her fingers tracing the edge of the table. "I just don't know, Dave," she said, her voice hesitant. "I'm not sure if I can keep up with you."

He turned toward her, his brow furrowing in confusion. "What do you mean?"

Nancy looked away; her eyes seemed distant as she spoke. "I don't know. This place…" she hesitated. "You always said that you came here because you wanted something different, something better. But now it feels like you're just… settling." She sighed, rubbing her temples. "I probably should have said something a while ago. But I've been too busy raising kids to sort this shit out in my head."

Her words stung. The truth was that their relationship had been on his mind as well. She wasn't wrong. He had been settling into something that pushed her out to the edges. And in doing so, he had built walls between the two of them.

"You may be right," he said slowly. "But none of this is meant to hurt you, Nancy. You know that, right?"

She sat there for a long moment, staring into space trying to come to terms with everything. Finally, she exhaled, her shoulders slumping slightly. "I know…" she said, her voice quieter now. "…but it's like you don't need me anymore. Like you're… okay without me."

Dave felt her words burrow deep into his chest. *It wasn't true.* Or maybe, he didn't want it to be true. But somewhere along the way, he had become so wrapped up in the business and the people who passed through, that he had forgotten how important she was in giving his life a purpose that wasn't entirely selfish.

Before he could respond, Nancy stood up abruptly, her chair scraping loudly against the floor. "I'm going to bed," she said softly. "You'll figure it out, David. You always do."

CHAPTER 16

YOU CAN TAKE THE MAN OUT OF THE FOREST

**"Cuz if I'm being honest the whole damn state
seems to be stuck back in the '70's
I know that just ended
but I feel like it might be that way for decades"**

(1996)

Dave glanced up from behind the counter as the door creaked open and Veiko's weathered face appeared. As always, he had a thermos under his arm, with his slow gait betraying the weight of years spent working his land.

It had been the same every Saturday around 5 p.m. since Dave bought the sauna almost two decades earlier. The woodsman would arrive alone, and trade pleasantries about the Red Sox before the conversation inevitably shifted to Veiko's true passions: trees, chainsaws, splitters—anything related to the forest.

Dave didn't know all the details, but he had pieced together that older man's life was simple and fully rooted in West Paris, where he'd been born and raised. A true Finn at heart, Veiko loved coffee, saunas, and the woods—in that order.

"Morning, Veiko!" Dave called jokingly, as the older man took his usual seat in the corner. The woodsman acknowledged him with a grunt, but didn't offer his customary nod or a smile, only a small, almost imperceptible frown tugging at the corners of his mouth.

Dave raised an eyebrow, unfamiliar with the woodsman displaying anything but an unchanged stoicism. "What's going on?" he asked, noticing the way his friend's shoulders were even more hunched than usual. "Trouble in the woods?"

Veiko sat down slowly, placing the thermos on the table, before releasing a sigh—a rare sign of weariness. He focused instead on successfully pouring coffee into the lid and took his time responding. "No, no trouble," Veiko muttered. "Just... tired, I guess. "Tired of being alone, Dave. It's... it's just me and the forest every day. And the trees are starting to crowd me."

Dave frowned. This wasn't the Veiko he knew. After all, this was a man who could talk for hours about the best way to fell a spruce tree or the intricacies of a Stihl chainsaw. Never before had he given any indication that something was bothering him.

Dave was caught off guard. His friend's whole life seemed wrapped in that quiet, rugged isolation—working the land, chopping wood, and keeping to himself. The idea that he was longing for something more was in some ways unsettling, if not entirely predictable.

"I never thought I'd hear you say that!" Dave said slowly, trying to gauge the seriousness in his friend's tone. "I figured you liked the quiet."

Veiko's face softened. "It's certainly peaceful," he said, staring into his coffee. "But now, all I hear is the wind and the silence, and it feels like it's pressing in on me, even suffocating me!"

Dave was momentarily at a loss for words. He had always admired Veiko's self-sufficiency, and hearing a vulnerability in his voice, was a bit disorienting. "You're out there in the woods every day, though," Dave said, trying to make sense of it. "Doesn't that fill the void? I mean, you're doing what you love."

Veiko chuckled bitterly. "That's the problem. It used to. But now, every day feels the same. I go out, cut my trees, take them out with the skidder, load them on trucks, and then... it's just me. I come back to an empty house. And that's it. Day after day."

Dave thought for a moment, scratching his chin. "OK" he said, looking out the window at the snow swirling outside. "I guess being alone isn't always as peaceful as people think."

Veiko looked up, eyes sharp with sudden interest. "You ever feel like that, Dave?... like there's nobody?"

Dave hesitated. Between his kids, his wife, and the lovers he took, there always seemed to be somebody. But he didn't think it made sense to share his good fortune with his friend at that moment and he spared him the truth.

"Yeah, sometimes. I mean, with the sauna, I'm rarely alone. But you can be surrounded by people, even family, and still feel like something's missing."

Veiko stared at him, considering. "Exactly. That's what it feels like. It's not about the work anymore or the quiet. It's about having someone to share them with. Cuz right now that silence is growing unbearable."

———

Veiko had always been a man who prided himself on keeping his electric bill under ten dollars a month and his daily life was a study in frugality. Dave had seen it firsthand after buying the sauna, when Veiko insisted on being grandfathered in and paying no more than $2 per visit. Dave wasn't usually one to back down on a dollar, especially with rumors swirling that the guy might secretly be a millionaire. But the woodsman had earned his special status, and Dave had relented.

Over the years, talking with Veiko had given Dave a much greater understanding of how central the forest was to both the local economy and culture. The woodsman's father had emigrated from Finland when he was young, and his son had grown up applying the lessons he'd learned from him. Spruce, Pine, Birch, Alder, Bears, Moose, Loons—apart from Maple, the Maine woods weren't much different from the forests of Finland. And even though chainsaws had replaced axes, and skidders had replaced horses, the core principles of working the land remained the same, whether in North America or Europe.

Despite the shift in the timber and paper industries over the last few decades, people in Maine were still heating their homes with wood, and wealthy people from away still enjoyed roaring fires at their ski lodges. That meant there was still plenty of money to be made from small woodlots.

Dave leaned back in his chair, folding his arms. "Sounds like you gotta find someone to share your life with!"

Veiko's face darkened again. "I don't know. I'm not sure what I have to offer. I've got my land, my cabin, and my tools. That's about it."

"You've got more than you think," Dave said, giving a small shrug. "You've got your health, your independence…and your own teeth. At your age that makes you quite a catch!" he concluded with a joking smile.

His friend took a long sip of his coffee, letting the steam rise between them. Finally, he sighed skeptically. "I just don't know if anyone is really going to want to join me in this life. Plus…where can I possibly find a woman around here? All the good ones are taken, and the rest expect me to go to church on Sundays. I'm not wasting my only day of rest on prayer."

Dave smiled, leaning forward. "Maybe you're not looking in the right places."

Veiko glanced up at him, eyebrow raised. "What do you mean?

"Who says she must be from around here? What about… online?" Dave replied.

The woodsman's eyes narrowed, a skeptical frown crossing his face. "Online? Are you serious?"

"Yeah, I am. There are women all over who'd appreciate the quiet life. Give it a shot!"

Veiko snorted, clearly not sold. "I don't even own a computer?"

"I do," Dave said, laughing. "Let me show you. You're never too old for this kind of thing." He pulled out a laptop computer which he used for day trading and after a few moments of resistance, the woodsman reluctantly sat down beside him. "Match.com. There are a lot of people looking for what you've got: space, nature, peace."

Veiko groaned. "This is a waste of time."

But before long Dave had set up a profile for Veiko with a bio highlighting his love of nature and a few flattering pictures of him with his chainsaw. He even made a note about how his cabin was always stocked with dry firewood.

"Now," Dave said, "all you have to do is wait."

———

Weeks passed, and Veiko found himself anticipating the strange routine of checking his online profile every Saturday at the sauna. And very much to his surprise, every week found new messages waiting for him—women from all over the country, all either intrigued by the simple life he led, or with a weakness for the on-line rustic charm that Dave had infused his profile with.

"She's the one! Her name's Maria." the woodsman insisted, pointing to a picture of a woman sitting on a John Deere tractor. "It says she has roots in Finland, a deep love for the woods, and the stillness of nature. She sounds like my cup of tea, and I'm a sucker for a woman in overalls!"

For the next half hour Dave helped him construct an email laying out all the advantages of life in western Maine, and enough of his buddy's backstory to give Maria something to think about. After reviewing his own writing, Dave handed the computer to the older man and showed him the send button.

"Here goes nothing," Veiko said stoically, before clicking on the button.

———

Driving home after his sauna, the older man could already feel the weight of his solitary existence slowly lifting from his shoulders. After a lifetime spent alone, it felt good to consider the possibility of forest solitude being entirely bearable. All it required was someone was waiting for him at home each night.

CHAPTER 17

OH NANCY

I know you've been hearing that I went astray
But that's just people talking, it's the small-town way
I may not be perfect, whatever that means
But don't listen to gossip, it's not what it seems"

(1998)

Returning from an early evening trip to the grocery store, Nancy arrived back to the sauna and found her husband enthusiastically engaged with a smiling brunette who was attempting to play pool. It was a familiar scene, on constant rotation for almost twenty years, and by now she was almost numb to it. But it still stung when it was happening right in front of her, and she immediately headed down the hall, away from people.

Dave caught her departure out of the corner of his eye, and he followed her towards the back, finally intercepting her outside of one of the sauna rooms. "C'mon Nancy…I'm just trying to be friendly…that's my job!" he said defensively. There was no trace of an apology in his voice.

"Does your job require getting their phone numbers?" Nancy asked, stopping sharply, and pointing directly at the script of paper in his hand.

Dave stared at the paper which provided him the few seconds he needed to cover his tracks. "She just wants a couple of cords," he said dismissively. Technically of course this was true, and Dave felt confident with his answer.

But Nancy knew the game he was playing. "If she needs wood, maybe she should ask her husband for it!" She was too smart to ignore the obvious and she knew it would just be a matter of time before his wood delivery became more than just innuendo.

Dave moved towards his wife and pulled her closer. "C'mon Nancy, you know I love you. I married you…and you're not even Italian," he said smiling. "A woman as beautiful as you? I had to move fast!"

He had imagined that the lack of space between them would work to his advantage, and he would be able to head off any kind of major confrontation. At the very least, he guessed it would help to minimize the damage. This strategy had worked well with previous transgressions, and he was hoping that twenty years hadn't dulled his ability to control the dialogue.

But Nancy pushed him away with a certainty that surprised both of them. "It's not you I worry about David! It's that thing between your legs…he's got a life of his own!" she said, pointing directly at his crotch. "And I'm not even that jealous of them. I just don't want the whole world knowing our business. And I don't want people looking at me like I'm stupid or oblivious…I'm neither!" She felt a familiar resentment creeping into her voice as the old scars burned again.

"No one thinks you're stupid. And anyways you shouldn't care what anyone else thinks. I sure don't!" Dave replied with a certainty backed up by twenty-five years of living by that creed.

Nancy knew this was all true enough. But *it wasn't about him*, and his inability to empathize frustrated her even more than the number exchange had.

"Yeah well…" she stumbled with her words, "… it's easy for you David. You're a guy. You get all the fun and few of the consequences. It's not like that for women. We get held to a whole different set of judgements and we gotta live with all the mess…it's not a fucking game for us." She was defiant and she moved farther away from her husband. Dave remained still, trying to figure out a workable pivot, and carefully slipping the paper back into his pocket.

Nancy continued out through the backdoor of the sauna and

took a gulp of clean air as she entered the cinderblock woodshed that sheltered neatly packed stacks of cordwood, and 55-gallon metal drums filled with kindling. She felt an immediate wave of relief washing over her body uncertain whether it was the result of getting away from the heated sauna rooms or simply getting away from her husband. Either way, it felt nice, and she continued through the shed before emerging in front of the Little Androscoggin River bordering the back of the sauna property.

The chill in the air mirrored Nancy's mood, and she couldn't help but notice that lately, she'd been spending more and more time imagining herself away from the sauna. Reaching around one of the barrels that was sitting in the yard, she grabbed a coffee can hidden behind it. She pulled out a cigarette from the pack inside and lit it. As the nicotine hit her system, her anger slowly gave way to a quiet melancholy.

It was becoming clear to her that she was no longer feeling the connection for the sauna, or if she was being honest, for the guy who owned it.

———

"What's wrong with you Nancy?" Dave said aggressively as he stepped out into the backyard.

"What's wrong with me David? What's wrong with you. I'm supposed to be your wife. But you're chasing women right in front of me, like I'm not even here. You moved us into that goddamn ridiculous house…you never even asked me whether I wanted to live in that monstrosity!" she continued referencing his most recent transgression; their family's relocation to a house located west down Rt. 26 that featured two large Romanesque columns in the front entrance and was known sarcastically as the *Mansion on the Hill*.

"I thought you liked that house," Dave said genuinely confused.

"Where the fuck did you get the idea that I liked that house?" Nancy replied defiantly. "And if all that's not bad enough…. I got fired today!" she blurted out.

"What?"

"They found out I was married to you, David. And now I'm done!" Nancy screamed at her husband.

For the past few months, Nancy had been employed in the brand-new position of Victims' Advocate at the Oxford County Courthouse. It was a position she had secured after a year and a-half of driving down to Westbrook College for paralegal classes.

The workload had been a lot to handle, especially with two kids still in school. But once she landed the job, she had felt a renewed sense of purpose, and had even gotten a taste of financial independence, something that had always felt out of reach for her.

And Nancy was good at the work. Her clients were mostly women, usually walking in scared, nervous, dejected, and ashamed. She had a gift for putting them at ease and getting them to open up with their stories. She also had the resourcefulness to help the victims find solutions to the problems they faced, either through official or if necessary, unofficial channels.

"Fuck them!" Dave asserted. "You should sue!" He was already envisioning a nice pay out for wrongful dismissal. "They're gonna need a better reason than that to fire you."

"No…they don't. The position was at-will for the first six months. So, they don't need any cause!" Nancy said dejectedly. She had been proud of what she had accomplished on her own and to watch it all disappear because of Dave's reputation, hurt her immensely and only reminded her of how tethered she had become to his legacy.

"Whatever. You can get another job." Her husband said, much too casually for his wife's taste.

"That's not the fucking point David! I don't want another job! I want the fucking job I had!" she screamed within inches of his face, before angrily retreating back inside the building.

———

Driving home alone, Nancy felt something permanent settling in. She was too old, too sad, and too tired for this.

It was time to leave Dave and the sauna in the rearview mirror.

CHAPTER 18

I'M A ROOSTER, YOU'RE A DOVE

**"So, we'll go out like the power
On a cold winter's night
No street sign to show us
What's next in this life"**

(1999)

Nancy stood beneath the grand pillars at the front of the house—the one she and Dave had called home for the past few years. She'd always found the extravagant design amusing, and so out of place in the quiet hills of western Maine. Her amusement had now shifted to a deep sense of discomfort, and she knew without question, that it was no longer where she wanted to be.

She stifled a bitter laugh, wondering if Dave's mother, Queenie, would ever let her son sell the only *real* home she considered him ever having, after leaving his parent's house nearly thirty years ago.

Nancy was certain she was done. For years—longer than she cared to admit—her own intuition and the advice of friends had urged her to walk away from Dave. His infidelity and selfishness had worn her thin, and now, she was finally ready to acknowledge that leaving him was the right thing to do.

But she was still a mother and so she had waited until their daughter, Heidi, had finished high school. A small part of her had held onto the hope that once her youngest left home, things might improve between them. But instead of rediscovering a connection, the emptiness of her own life had become all too clear after their youngest moved out.

The final straw came when Dave began withholding money from her. Over the past six months, a friend of Nancy's had started buying cocaine from him on a regualr basis—first an ounce, then two, then five, and eventually fifteen. The arrangement had turned into a profitable deal for Dave. In exchange for the connection, he promised Nancy *a bullet* for each ounce her friend bought.

With a resale value of nearly four hundred dollars per, Nancy had finally been on track to make enough money to gain some financial independence. But he already owed her for more than 75 bullets, and his hostility had only grown as she pressed him to honor his part of the deal.

But sensing her withdrawal, Dave was now refusing to bankroll her departure.

———

Nancy headed down to the basement, retrieved her luggage, and returned upstairs where she set it on the bed. She still had several hours before her husband would be home, but she was anxious to leave. She knew the longer she waited, the more likely she was to talk herself out of it—or, even worse, get caught in a confrontation.

As she moved from room to room scanning the contents, she realized—much to her surprise—that there was nothing in the house she felt attached to. *Not a damn thing here I want*, she thought to herself, pulling up a chair at the kitchen table. She took a pen from her purse and began to write, carefully selecting her words in what was likely to be a vain attempt to keep things civil.

After a half hour of agonizing over the letter, Nancy finally felt that she had gotten it right. She placed the note on the table, grabbed a few photo albums she'd put together over the years, and took one last look around the house. After climbing into her van, she headed to her sisters who had offered her a trailer in her backyard for the time being.

Driving north on Route 26, the radio blasted WBLM out of Portland, and Jackson Browne's *Running on Empty* become the soundtrack of her escape. As tears streamed down her face, she found herself stifling a laugh as she imagined herself the start of her own music video.

Now, all she had to figure out was how to break the news to her parents, who had always liked her husband—especially since he'd been so generous with loans, at a reasonable twenty percent interest.

———————

Much later that evening, Dave arrived back at the house and found Nancy's letter sitting on the table. He picked up the paper, and felt a sickening feeling settle in his stomach. He reluctantly sat down at the table and opened the folded letter.

Dear David,

On more than one occasion you told me if ever I wasn't happy then I should get out. That's what I am doing. This is not an easy decision and it's also not a sudden decision. For more than a few years it has been clear (probably to both of us) that who you are and who I am, are no longer compatible. Please understand I am not condemning who you are, but I need to fend for myself. At this point in my life, I want a partner who remains devoted to me and who I am enough for. I no longer want to share my husband with any good-looking girl who comes into the sauna.

As much as I love you, it's obvious that I can't keep you happy....

Dave stopped reading and violently ripped up the paper before depositing it in the trash. *Fuck this*, he screamed silently, and his head started spinning. He began frantically zigzagging around the house, checking to see what Nancy had taken as part of her departure.

After a few minutes of searching, he realized that outside of the clothes she owned, it appeared that his wife had left everything behind. On a practical level he was relieved that nothing seemed to be missing. But it hurt him to see it made so obvious, that the house and everything in it, were of no importance to Nancy.

———

Dave sat at the kitchen table late into the night, where his mood alternated between anger and his real-world concern as to what this would mean for his finances. He knew the nature of his business enterprises made him extremely vulnerable to an ex-wife with a grudge. And even though Nancy wasn't the vindictive type, any attorney worth their salt was certainly going to push for a full accounting of Dave's finances and real estate holdings. And that kind of scrutiny, was not going to work in his favor.

He knew he would need to move quickly if he was going to protect his assets. He hadn't risked breaking so many laws over the years, just to have it all taken from him by some lawyer.

———

The MC clubhouse buzzed with nervous energy, —like the hum of an electric fence waiting to snap. Nearly three dozen men, the heart of the club, sat around the worn wooden tables, leaning in close, talking just above a whisper. It was unusual for the place to feel this tense, with the norm usually being laughter and perhaps a few loud arguments over poker hands. But today, the conversation was serious and hushed, like there was a third presence in the room, watching, waiting.

"Goddamn it," Donnie muttered, his fingers drumming nervously against the tabletop. "I didn't think it would go this far."

Across from him, Razor leaned back in his chair, arms crossed, eyes hard. "What did you expect? He's been with her how long? Twenty years? C'mon. She's probably been tired of this shit for a long time."

Donnie's eyes flicked up to meet Razor's. "If she drags him

down, she drags all of us down with him."

T-Bone, who'd been silent up until now, leaned forward, his chair scraping the floor as he set his elbows on the table. "She knows too much, man. She's been listening to all our bullshit for years. The way we talk when we're too drunk to think straight, when we forget who might be around. She's got enough ammo to turn the whole goddamn club inside out, including all the photo's she was always taking."

"I've heard rumors," Jackal chimed in from the far end of the room, his voice bitter. "They're saying she's gonna tell the feds everything. Hell, maybe they already got her on the line. If she's out for revenge, we're dead in the water. We've already got a half dozen law enforcement agencies breathing down our necks!"

"Easy, Jackal," Razor growled, his eyes narrowing. "We don't need you running around scaring everyone more than they already are."

Jackal didn't back down. "I'm just sayin'—she's not some innocent woman in this. She knows what's been going on, and she's been here long enough to see everything. If she thinks he's gonna screw her over, she's going to do whatever it takes to get her piece."

A low murmur spread across the room, the weight of Jackal's words sinking in. The bikers exchanged tense glances, and there was a temporary silence, before T-Bone spoke.

"We gotta figure out what she's gonna do," he said, breaking the silence. "If she goes to the authorities, it's not just his ass on the line. It's the whole club. Everything we've built, everything we've worked for... gone."

Silence returned to the room. Only a decade ago, one of their own MC brothers had given up a couple of their biker buddies after the promise of a plea deal and walked out of prison after only a few years. It had taken a while for the club to get back on their feet after that hit, and a whole lot of friendships had been erased overnight. It wasn't something that any of the men wanted to experience again.

T-Bone turned to Donnie, "You still banging the secretary over at the lawyer's office?" he asked.

"Naah, not for a few months now, but we're still on good terms," Donnie insisted. "I'll give her a call and see what I can find out. In the meantime, let's keep our distance until we see where this lands."

———

In a dimly lit office on Main St. in South Paris, Hal Berry, Nancy's lawyer, was pushing her to take the easy way out. "Tell them Dave's a drug dealer," he insisted. "They'll lock him up, and you walk away unscathed, with all his assets. You get to start over, and you'll be set for life."

Nancy listened politely, but the idea of betraying her ex, left a sour taste in her mouth. She didn't hate Dave. She hated what he'd done to her, sure. But she wasn't going to put him in prison. And there was something else nagging at her—something her attorney was forgetting: *If he goes down, they'll seize everything. She won't see a penny of it.* She'd have to start from scratch, and after two decades in, that wasn't something she was willing to do, no matter how much she currently resented him.

———

Back at the clubhouse, Hal's secretary arrived—a woman who'd dated several of the members over the years and who had continued feeding the club information on anything of interest that passed through the attorney's office.

"They're saying she won't play ball," Hal's secretary asserted. "She's not gonna turn on him."

The room seemed to exhale as one.

Razor let out a low chuckle. "Well, I'll be damned. I didn't think she had it in her. We'll take it."

———

There was some obvious tension in the courtroom as Dave and

Nancy sat across from each other. Dave had been too cheap to hire a lawyer, but he had come to court wearing a suit. His eyes darted nervously between the judge, the court stenographer, and Nancy's attorney, who sat next to her, his sharp suit and perfect posture a stark contrast to Dave's disheveled appearance.

Judge Thompson, an older man with a furrowed brow and glasses that seemed perpetually perched at the end of his nose, was glancing down at his notes, with a perplexed look on his face. He looked over at Dave who had just finished presenting his case.

"So, Mr. Graiver," Judge Thompson said, his voice laced with a touch of amusement, "you're arguing that $4 million in assets should be exempt from division because they come from a personal gift you received years before your marriage?"

"That's correct, Your Honor," Dave said, puffing out his chest slightly, trying to maintain an air of confidence despite the skeptical glances he was getting from everyone in the room.

"And this gift—these treasury bonds—were given to you when, exactly?" the judge asked.

"Thirty-five years ago, Your Honor, for my Bar Mitzvah. It was a personal gift from my grandmother. I was only twelve at the time. It wasn't tied to any business venture or illegal activity."

There was a ripple of muted laughter from the gallery. Hal Berry's lips twitched into a half-smile, and even Judge Thompson had to hide the curve of his mouth behind his hand. Dave, oblivious to the subtle mockery, continued.

"I've invested the money wisely over the years, Your Honor, and it's grown. But it still belongs to me. It's personal. It's not community property."

Judge Thompson adjusted his glasses, raising an eyebrow. "Interesting legal theory, Mr. Graiver. I'll humor you for a moment." He glanced over at Hal. "Mr. Berry, care to respond?"

The attorney leaned forward, the corners of his mouth turning downward into a professional frown. His tone was calm, measured, but there was a glint of amusement in his eyes. "Your Honor, with all due respect to Mr. Graiver, I think we can agree that $4 million doesn't exactly resemble the gift he received from his grandparent as a twelve-year-old. It's clear that this is simply an attempt to shield marital assets from equitable division."

"Objection, Your Honor," Dave interjected, holding up a hand, his voice high-pitched and defensive. "That's speculative! My grandmother's gift has been in my name for years. That didn't change after I got married.

The judge leaned forward, his fingers steepled together. "Mr. Graiver, I'm going to make this clear: the presumption in a divorce case is that all assets accumulated during the marriage are subject to division, unless they can be proven to be separate property. You've presented no evidence, that these treasury bonds and the money you've made off them are not marital assets."

Dave's face flushed. "My grandmother gave them to me. It was a gift. A personal gift that I have left alone for decades, before and after the marriage."

Hal shot a look at the judge, and then back at Dave, his voice dripping with sarcasm. "So, your argument, Mr. Gravier, is that your entire $4 million came from a Bar Mitzvah gift? That seems, well... interesting, to say the least."

The judge cleared his throat, his eyes glimmering with barely contained amusement. "Mr. Gravier, I'm going to be honest with you. I've heard many arguments in my career, but that one is certainly a first. However, your legal theory has not convinced me that these assets should be exempt from the marital estate."

Dave's jaw tightened. "But I—"

Hal was already standing up, his voice smooth as silk as he addressed the judge. "Your honor, if I may, we have other evidence the court can consider if it wants to continue wasting its time on the defendants frivolous legal claims. If need be we can submit evidence showing that these bonds, while technically separate property, have been manipulated during the marriage to obscure their value."

Dave's eyes widened. "That's... that's not true! I haven't hidden anything! Everything's on the books—just because I moved things around doesn't mean—"

"Mr. Gravier," Judge Thompson interrupted, his tone firm, "this is not yet a criminal trial. However, I must admit, your method of managing finances is... unorthodox."

There was a brief, uncomfortable pause, and Dave felt his chest tighten. Hal moved to submit the evidence, and the judge looked over at Dave.

"But—but I—" Dave started, but Judge Thompson cut him off with a raised hand.

"I've heard enough, Mr. Graiver. I'll issue my decision in writing, but suffice to say, I'm not inclined to accept your argument that $4 million of assets should be exempt from the division just because of a Bar Mitzvah gift."

Dave slumped slightly, his shoulders sagging. He shot a glance at Nancy, who was holding back a satisfied smile. Hal, on the other hand, was barely containing a grin as he gathered his papers.

"Thank you, your honor," The lawyer said, standing up straight, his voice smooth. "We'll await the official ruling, but we're confident in the outcome."

The judge nodded, "Court adjourned!" slamming his gavel down with a sharp bang.

As the sound echoed through the courtroom, Dave returned to his chair. His chest felt heavy with the possibly of $4 million slipping away from him. *Still though, at least they missed most of the real estate*, he thought, and a smile returned to his face.

———

"But that's not my problem...I still need you to pay your rent!"

I'M A ROOSTER, YOU'RE A DOVE

A few days after the trial verdict, Dave was sitting comfortably in his chair slurping up a large bowl of cereal and urgently trying to track down payment from a tenant who was late with the rent. Through the window he watched his wife's car pull up outside. She was followed by the familiar brown and white colors of an Oxford County Sheriff's vehicle. "No, you gotta bring it to the sauna!" He hung up the phone so he could assess what appeared to be a more pressing situation.

"Sorry, David," Nancy said as she made her way into the sauna. She was accompanied by Roger Bell, one of the local sheriff's deputies, who was a long-time regular at the sauna.

"What the fuck is this, Nancy?" his ex-husband asked angrily. He turned towards the deputy and calmly said, "Hey Roger!" The deputy nodded sheepishly. Dave had always been good to him during his sauna visits, and he humbly retreated towards the door, realizing it might be best to stay out of Dave's vision. At least until Nancy's attorney arrived. The last thing he wanted was to risk a ban from the place.

After more than a few minutes of uncomfortable silence, the lawyer finally pulled up, and the deputy was forced back to work. Dave glared at both Nancy and her Attorney Berry, but remained seated, seemingly unaware of why they were even there.

"It's behind over there" Nancy said to her attorney, pointing to the unfinished counter of rough-cut lumber sitting in the foreground. For a moment nobody moved, and another awkward silence came over the room. Finally, the sheriff's deputy walked back behind the counter.

"It's here," the deputy acknowledged. "Hey Dave, any chance you could just open it for us?"

"Does your court order compel me to?" Dave inquired.

The deputy looked in the direction of Attorney Berry, who shook his head.

"I'll get some tools from the back of my vehicle," the deputy said and headed back outside.

Ten minutes later, Roger had managed to separate the safe from the shelving built under the counter. The deputy slowly pulled it out into the middle of the room and put a piece of paperwork on the top for Dave to sign.

Dave looked over at Nancy and shook his head. But he went ahead and signed the paper.

"Can we just open it here?" Nancy asked her attorney. "I don't really want a safe in my trailer."

"It's your property now. So, you can do whatever you want with it!" her attorney replied, sounding annoyed at the question.

"How about you just open it for me David?" Nancy pleaded. "I just want what's inside." She calculated that in the end, he would prefer not having to buy a new safe.

Grudgingly her ex-husband moved to the safe, shielded his hands, and began dialing the combination. Once he had it set, he turned the handle and stepped back.

Nancy and her attorney made their way to the front of the safe and pulled open the door. A pile of what appeared to be papers were set on the one shelf inside.

Nancy let out a disappointed sigh. She had hoped that the safe would be stuffed to capacity with cash. Even ten or fifteen thousand dollars would go a long way toward helping her build her new life. Now the best she could hope for was that these documents might provide information leading to money or assets that Dave had hidden somewhere.

It was only after Hal laid out the contents of the safe on the pool table that Nancy realized that what was in front of her. Photographs. Of her. Naked.

"You're a bastard!" Nancy screamed at her ex-husband. "Keep your fucking safe!" She grabbed the photos and hastily exited the sauna, followed by her attorney and the sheriff's deputy.

Dave picked up his bowl of cereal and returned to his chair. He was going to miss those photos.

CHAPTER 19

I DO BANKING
IN MY SHORTS

**"They got their homes, they got their banks
And stocks and bonds to fill their tanks
I do my banking in my shorts
And bury barrels in the woods"**

(2001)

Dave settled into his seat on the plane, his shoulders relaxing as he glanced over at the older couple sharing his row. They didn't seem the type to make small talk or try to turn the flight into some forced bonding experience, and for that, he was grateful. After all, he was leaving his first real vacation in twenty years with no real clarity on where to go from here. As the plane ascended into the skies and headed back to the quiet familiarity of Maine, he urgently hoped that springtime had made at least a subtle appearance.

When he left for the Bahamas back in November, it had felt like the perfect escape—a potential cure for the mental and emotional chaos he had been trying to drown in cocaine for a few years. The idea of sun-soaked days, sand between his toes, margaritas by the beach, and women in bikinis seemed like exactly what he needed.

And for a few months, he'd been swept up in the illusion. A new life, away from it all. No more snowstorms to shovel out from. No more nosy neighbors whispering behind his back. No angry, ex-wife sending texts messages. Hell, even the IRS couldn't track him down with his shell companies all carefully hidden under a fake name. began to imagine selling off the sauna, liquidating all the properties

He still owned in Maine, and spending the rest of his life living the dream—endless sunshine, no obligations, no reminders of what he used to be.

Visits from his kids had also been a welcome distraction as they joined him for snorkeling trips, bike rides along the coastal roads, and one memorable weeklong bender with Lennie and his fiancée. But as they shared their interactions with Nancy, it only reinforced for him that he was now a divorcee. Even more difficult was that his kids were eager to know who this version of their father had become, and he didn't have any answers.

After a few months in, Dave started feeling like a coward, like a cliché. The kind of guy who traded in his real life for a pair of sunglasses, a Panama hat, and a bar stool in Nassau. And as the months passed, the disquiet inside him grew, and he realized that if he didn't make a change soon, he'd become the punchline of a bad joke.

As the clock ticked, his mind had drifted back to Maine. There, at least, the seasons changed, predictably. But for a while, the thought of going back had made him uneasy. It would demand a reckoning that he wasn't sure he was prepared for.

But now his brief attempt to outrun the world was coming to an end. It was time.

———

Dave winced as he made quick work of a bowl of cereal. The colder Maine weather had also meant the return of all the joint pain that island weather had masked. It would be a couple hours before the sauna rooms would be up to temperature and for a moment he wondered if coming back had been a wise decision.

And something else was off, he just hadn't been able to put his finger on it.

The money, he realized suddenly. His stomach twisted. He was pretty sure he had hidden a large amount of it in one of the

50-gallon metal barrels out back before leaving for his recent island vacation. But now... where?

He grabbed a coat and marched out into the yard. The wind was sharp enough to make him squint. His boots crunched through the dead grass as he approached the first barrel, and the metal was cold against his hand as he shook it. Empty.

He moved to the next one. Same story. He threw another handful of scrap wood to the ground, eyes darting around the yard, frantic.

Ten barrels later, Dave's heart was racing. He felt like he was losing his mind, and he was in full panic mode. He hadn't been alive long enough to start forgetting things like this.

"Goddamn it!" he muttered under his breath. "Maybe I buried it!" He had no clear memory, but it was how he usually did it.

He picked up the phone and dialed his his son.

"Dad? What's going on?" Lennie's voice crackled over the line.

"Lennie, I—I buried money before I left," Dave stammered, already feeling ridiculous. "And now - now I can't remember where. It's gone. I swear to God, I thought I put it here —"

"Dad, breathe. I'll be up in a few hours to help look."

Dave hung up and stood there for a moment, hands on his hips. *I should have stayed in the fucking Bahamas!*

———————

A few hours later, Lennie arrived, and the search party began. His youngest son, Walter, had also rolled up with his excavator, and together they all moved out to the backyard.

"Dad, this is going to be a disaster," Walter muttered as he revved the engine, his brow furrowed. "You sure it's out here?"

"It has to be," his father said through gritted teeth, staring at the uneven ground.

Minutes passed and the machine began digging into the soft earth, tossing up mounds of dirt that quickly made the yard resemble a battlefield. Dave knew he only had a small window to re-fill the dug-up holes before the neighbor used it as an excuse to call in the DEP for some kind of shoreline violation.

Weird Rob approached from behind, wearing a sagging T-shirt and sunglasses that were clearly too dark for the late afternoon.

"I've got news," Weird Rob said in his gravelly voice. "Nancy was at the sauna a few weeks ago. She was hanging around a lot while you were gone."

Dave froze. "Was she?" His voice was low. Had he been blind to something obvious?

Weird Rob continued. "I'm just saying, she was here. She knew the place. Could have figured out where you hid it."

The thought made Dave's stomach flip. His ex-wife. The woman who'd just finished shredding his life, and now possibly, the one to betray him once and for all.

He moved out of the vicinity of his sons and began dialing her number with shaking hands. It rang a couple time before a familiar voiced picked up.

"Hello?" Nancy's voice came through, cool and dismissive.

"Did you take it?" her ex-husbands words tumbled out. "Did you take the money while I was gone?"

"What are you talking about, David?" She sounded bored. "I came by to use the sauna, that's all. I didn't take anything. I just wanted to avoid you… after what happened last time—"

"I wasn't going to run you over," he interrupted, gritting his teeth.

"You scared me, Dave. You know that, right? Anyway, I didn't take your damn money. Whatever's gone, you're on your own." She hung up before he could respond.

Dave stared at the cell phone in his hand, feeling a deep frustration building inside him. All the old habits—the tricks, the games he'd played to stay one step ahead of the law, his ex-wife, even himself—seemed pointless now. The money was probably gone. But that was hardly the worst of it.

He was sensing now that the 1970's were finally ending in Maine, twenty years after it had ended for the rest of the country. Dave no longer knew who he could trust, and every part of his life seemed so much more complex. These had not been his intentions when he arrived thirty years ago.

As he listened to the hum of the excavator, Dave felt the crushing weight of regret, squeezing the air from his lungs. He wasn't just losing money. He was losing faith in his own ability to make the right decision.

And he had no idea how to get himself back on track.

CHAPTER 20

HOUSE RULES

"Long John Silver, the rumors were true, and
Hugh the Brit who'd sometimes pass through
One Armed Kim but that's all that it takes, and
Johnnie the Stripper with all his pet snakes
Boat sluts and coke whores and closeted men
Liars and cheaters who needed a friend"

(2002)

Memorial Day weekend was always a frenzy in western Maine. The air held the last remnants of spring, and the joyful sounds of locals shaking off the cold and tending to their gardens. Summer folks had also begun to trickle in—eager to open their camps, stretch out in the sun, and dive into their first taste of the season. The sauna was humming with energy and every room was taken.

For Dave, it was a mixed blessing. The chaos meant more work—more wood to stack, more towels to fold, more small talk to handle. But it also meant possibilities. An endless parade of people meant more chances for distraction—something to pull him out of the fog that had settled in his head after the divorce. A conversation here, a laugh there, maybe even someone who could make him forget, just a little bit.

Saturday afternoon proved no different and Dave was busy trying to stay ahead of the rush when he heard the door open with a light jingle. Stepping back into the lounge he saw two women arriving arm and arm. "Hey ladies," he said, flashing a friendly smile in their direction. He recognized one of the visitors from a previous visit but couldn't remember her name.

The taller one with short dark hair, who he had recognized, grinned back. "Hi Dave!"

Dave was at a loss, but she laughed and quickly rescued him. "Megan!" she said.

"Of course." He nodded toward her companion—a shorter woman with light brown hair. "And you are?"

"Sandy!" she replied, offering a soft smile. Her eyes were calm but suggestive and Dave found himself holding eye contact just a bit longer than usual. It quickly became a two-way conversation between them, with the usual small talk about the drive over and what she did for work.

Dave discovered that Sandy taught high school English in Portsmouth, and they were busy comparing their favorite authors when Weird Rob interrupted.

"Dave..." his timing was impeccable. "Something's up with the washer!" he shouted peaking his head into the lounge area.

"That fucking guy wouldn't know a washer if it hit him in the head," Dave whispered to Sandy. "I should probably deal with this. You and your friend should hang out after your sauna for a drink!" he suggested.

———

"You girls like to party?" he asked as Sandy and Megan rejoined him in the lounge area with towels wrapped around their heads.

The two women checked in with each other and simultaneously replied, "Sure!"

"Meet me out front in fifteen and you can follow me up to my house." Dave told them.

"We'll be ready!" Megan assured him as they headed back to their changing room.

Glancing over his shoulder, he caught a glimpse of Weird Rob making his way towards him and his stomach sank. *Fuck no!* Rob had been a steady presence at the sauna for a long time, but Dave didn't want to spend his off time hanging out with the guy and he knew he was going to request an invitation to the get-together.

He turned around and planted himself firmly in Weird Rob's path.

"Rob, I need you to stay here tonight. Watch the fires. I can't leave the place unattended."

Weird Rob's face fell, his shoulders sagging like he'd been physically struck. "You sure?" he asked, his voice flat, laced with disappointment.

"Yup!" Dave replied with a finality.

Weird Rob's lip twitched. Without another word, he turned and shuffled down the hallway.

Dave watched him go. He didn't want to hurt the guy. He never did. But tonight, he had other plans, and his tenant would just be the wrong kind of distraction.

After making a few phone calls and inviting a few of the other sauna customers, he headed out to his truck and found Megan and Sandy waiting in their vehicle. As the truck rolled forward, Dave glanced one last time at the front of the sauna, where Weird Rob was now keeping a lonely vigil in the window.

———

A short time later, the invited guests arrived at Dave's house and were confronted by some clear indicators that no women were currently living there. There was dirty laundry scattered across chairs and dishes still piled high on the counters, some of them sporting days-old food remnants that had long since hardened into grotesque, sticky patches.

The distinct scent of a bachelor's life—dejected, uninspired, and unwashed—hung in the air. None of which seemed to bother the group that had gathered, who all seemed eager to dive into the night.

Sandy felt an odd attraction to the chaos she had walked into. Dave was clearly the type of man who needed a little help and she had always had a weakness for men who needed fixing.

As the evening wore on, the energy in the house ramped up, and Sandy decided to sneak away for a bit of space. She'd heard a rumor about a hot tub upstairs, and after a few drinks, she was ready to investigate.

After quietly removing herself from the kitchen, she found the stairs heading to the second floor. At the top of the stairs, she turned to follow a narrow hallway leading to an open door at the end. Stepping into the room, Sandy found herself face to face with a well-used king-sized bed sitting lazily in the corner. Directly in front of it was a four-person jacuzzi, just daring someone to get in. The whole scene was straight out of any number of low-budget porn movies she had seen.

She stood there chuckling to herself before Dave's voice startled her from behind. "You want to try it?"

She spun around, to see him walking toward her, confidently peeling off his shirt. *Damn, he looks good!* she thought. Despite his age, Dave was in excellent shape—his muscles were well-defined, and the scars of time only added to the appeal. He was aging well.

Her heart skipped a beat, and she caught herself trying to maintain some level of control. Getting into a hot tub with a stranger hadn't been in her plan for the evening. Certainly, for the party, for the distraction, but now—now, she was being offered something a little more dangerous. She wondered how far she should take it.

But her mouth spoke before she could think better of it.

"Sure!"

Dave finished undressing, stepped into the tub, and hit the dimmer switch on the lights. The atmosphere shifted immediately—more intimate, more private.

Sandy hesitated for a moment, but it wasn't long before she had stripped down to her bra and panties and approached the hot tub.

"Uh, uh, uh," Dave said. "It's all gotta come off. House rules!"

She smiled and removed the rest of her clothing before climbing into the bubbling water. Sitting across from him, she positioned the jets so that her back got the most pressure, and sank into the warmth of the jacuzzi.

It was going to be a good night.

CHAPTER 21

MAKE ME AN OFFER

"So, make me an offer, I'm really no good at these things
Like a carousel rider who is always grasping for rings
I'd be a thousand miles from here if I had my wish
So, make me an offer, it's got to be better than this"

(2004)

Sandy lay on her bed in Portsmouth, with the soft glow of a lamp casting shadows across her room. She was flipping through the pages of a dog-eared romance novel she had read countless times—comfortably trashy, just the way she liked it. Her cell phone buzzed on the nightstand, and without bothering to even look at the incoming number, she answered it.

"I was hoping you'd call," she said with a playful voice as the line connected. "I'm getting sick of younger men," she added with a laugh, settling onto her side and propping her head up on her hand. "Especially the ones who still wet their pants!"

Dave chuckled on the other end. "What's got you worked up now?" he inquired.

Sandy exhaled, the frustration slipping into her voice. "It's my students. I feel like I'm wasting my time, you know? I gotta find something else. This is killing me!"

She was just getting started. "And the teachers with their cliques in the faculty lounge...the petty arguements...the passive-aggressive comments... It's exhausting. I'm surrounded by *children*, and most of them have degrees!"

"Yeah, I remember what it was like. I did my time," he reminded her. There was a trace of nostalgia in his voice.

Sandy let out a long breath. It felt good to vent to Dave. Over the last year and a half their relationship had evolved into something substantial and what had started as phone calls a couple times a week was now a nightly tradition, after the sauna closed.

After a pause, Dave spoke again. There was a hint of mischief in his voice. "Hey…" he said, "how about another trip to the sauna this weekend?"

Sandy didn't have to think. "Sure. Why not?"

———

"When are you going to pay me back?" Dave asked his oldest son as he emerged from the house with a couple of drinks in his hand.

"Pay you back for what?" Lennie retorted defiantly. But he knew what his dad was referring to, since he had been rehashing the joke to friends and family at least once a year, going all the way back to his son's childhood.

The story was that following his son's birth, Dave had found himself in a small office at the local hospital negotiating with a frustrated hospital official. The administrator was trying to figure out some kind of payment plan for a traumatic birthing that involved both expensive equipment and additional staffing.

Dave had remained steadfast in his declaration that he was a broke hippie homesteader with very little electricity and no steady job to draw payments from. After spending more than two hours trying to locate a source of income from the new father, the hospital ended up capitulating, and negotiating a payment plan with Dave that allowed him to pay $5 per month until the bill was repaid.

When Lennie had turned eighteen, Dave had handed his oldest son a bill along with a request that he take over payments for his own birth and reimburse his dad for the *long-term loan* he had covered for all these years.

"$1080 is what I put the principle at. With 12% interest over

36 years. I'll give you the family discount and call it an even 6k," Dave said earnestly. "And don't try to Jew me down! Also, next time you see your mother tell her she still hasn't paid her half of the bill either."

Lennie smiled. "You are so fucking cheap!"

"Hey, I need the extra income. I just asked Sandy to move in and she's got a healthy appetite," his father joked as he leaned against one of the pillars on the front porch.

"Are you going to live here?" his son asked.

"I'm going to sell it." Dave's words hung in the air. He stared off at the view of the property, the house that had once been a home now feeling like nothing more than a relic of another life. "I can't bring another woman here. Too many memories. Too much — *baggage*. I need a fresh start."

Lennie took a long pull from his beer, his eyes narrowing as he processed his father's words. This wasn't a surprise—he had seen it in Dave's eyes when he'd arrived. He had the look of a man in full transition, shedding skin and wanting to erase everything that came before. The divorce had hit his father hard, and his whole family was anxious to be done with that chapter in his life.

"You should go through the stuff in the garage," Dave added. "See if there's anything you want to keep. The rest of it... I'll handle it."

His son nodded, but the idea of rummaging through boxes of old photos, faded furniture, and forgotten memorabilia held no excitement for him. He'd never felt any real attachment to his dad's latest home. By the time the rest of the family had moved in, he'd already left for college in Bangor. He guessed even his siblings would probably feel the same way—there were very few memories here for any of them to hold onto.

The two of them let their gaze wander over the landscape. "Where are you and Sandy going to live?" Lennie asked.

It was hard to ignore the fact that his dad had been living in the back of a truck for the last few months, parked out in front of the sauna. But Dave seemed unfazed by it—and it was certainly the best low-cost alternative available.

A flash of a grin tugged at the corners of his mouth. The corners of his shoulders lifted slightly as though he'd just received a jolt of energy. "I'm building a condo!" he said with a mock flourish, a twinkle in his eye. "Right behind the sauna."

Lennie arched an eyebrow, incredulous. "A condo?"

Dave chuckled, the sound low and amused. "It's not *really* a condo," he clarified, glancing off toward the wooded stretch beyond the property. "But I'm building it, damn it!"

His son could already picture the result, and based on the frugal nature of his father, he guessed that the structure would be little more than a box with a mattress inside.

"And you're doing this without a permit?"

Dave waved a hand dismissively, the grin never fading. "I don't worry about that much. The code enforcement officer is still a regular. I'll get a little grace."

Lennie shook head. No matter how questionable his dad's methods might be, it was hard not to admire the way he threw himself into things with an almost reckless optimism.

The silence stretched between them for a moment before his oldest concluded the conversation. "Alright," he said, tipping his beer toward his dad. "I guess we'll see what comes of the condo then."

Dave nodded, taking a final swig of his beer before dropping the can on the ground.

By the time August rolled around, Sandy was ready take Dave up on his offer. She handed in her notice at the school in Portsmouth and before the ink had even dried on the resignation letter, she found herself with an offer from an understaffed alternative high school in Lewiston. It wasn't glamorous, but it felt real.

Thankfully, work had also finished on the new apartment behind the sauna, which had required illegally filling in a swampy section of his property. This had been successfully accomplished by relocating fill from the hill that divided the sauna from his neighbor's property.

"I used to daydream about living on a farm," Sandy murmured, as she and Dave shared a couple of beers on the newly constructed porch that he had also recently added to the back of the sauna. "Raising animals, growing things. But I've been stuck in cities my whole life."

Dave, who'd been telling her stories about his own days living in a farmhouse, smiled and took a long pull from his bottle. His body was tired from a day spent hauling firewood. "I get that," he said, his voice wistful. "I used to think about it, too. But the thing is, farming is messy, hard, and... not particularly profitable."

Sandy laughed softly, her lips curling up at the edges. "You've done well with it!"

Dave grinned and leaned back in his chair. "Well, I wasn't doing the farming. Just helping to distribute the produce," he laughed, adding a wink. "You're not going to catch me out there plowing fields anytime soon."

———

A few weeks later, Sandy decided to go south and visit her parents for the weekend, Dave saw the perfect opportunity to surprise her. With a little help from Weird Rob and a line or two from his personal medicine cabinet, he built a small livestock pen on the side of the sauna building. By the time Sandy's car came rolling into the gravel lot Sunday evening, she was met with the sound of bleating goats and the snorts of curious llamas.

As she stepped out of the car, her eyes widened. Dave stood off to the side, clearly pleased with himself, his grin wide and proud as he watched her approach.

Sandy took a few hesitant steps toward the fence. "What the hell is this?" she asked, her voice low, not quite believe what she was seeing.

"Two goats, two llamas, and three sheep. There is Elmer, Red, and Hazel," he said like he was introducing friends. Gesturing toward the fence. "Go ahead, take a look."

The animals, with their shaggy coats and wide eyes, were a surreal but welcoming sight. The goats were nibbling lazily at the grass while the llamas were giving her wary looks, like they were sizing her up. But it was the sheep—oh, the sheep—that made her laugh. Elmer, with his patchy wool and awkward stance. It was all both absurd, and charming.

"I can't believe you did this," Sandy murmured, still smiling. She looked at Dave, a half-laugh escaping her lips. "I swear, you're nuts. But this… this is perfect."

"I thought it'd be a nice surprise. Something different," he admitted with a chuckle.

Sandy leaned closer to the fence, reaching her hand through to scratch the back of Elmer's ears. "Well…" she said, still grinning, "…you certainly got my attention."

Unfortunately, the new structure had also gotten the attention of the next-door neighbor. As they stood admiring the animals, they spotted Bob scoping out the livestock pen, from a safe distance. Even from thirty yards away, they could see a disapproving frown tugging at his lips. He muttered something under his breath before turning on his heels and marching off.

"Uh oh," Sandy said, his voice tight with irritation. "You don't think he's gonna complain?"

"Bob?" Dave glanced over at the retreating figure of the neighbor. "He's probably already planning a petition."

Sandy looked at him, her expression shifting from amusement to concern. "You're sure about this? I mean, this is legal right?"

Dave laughed bitterly. "Not really. But I'm not going to let some grumpy old man tell me what I can do with my own property."

"Maybe we could make it work," Sandy suggested, her brow furrowing slightly. "We could apply for a permit or something?"

Dave shook his head. "We'll see. Permits aren't really my thing."

Sandy watched him for a moment before nodding slowly. "You really are stubborn, aren't you?"

Dave grinned. "I like to think of it as determination." He looked back at the pen, his eyes narrowing. "I'll find a way around this. I always do."

———

When the fines started adding up, Dave was finally forced to admit that the neighbor had won. On one of his other properties, far away from the prying eyes of the neighbor and the zoning board, he fenced in nine acres. Soon enough he had moved the animals to a place where they could roam free, without any complaints from people with too much time on their hands.

CHAPTER 22

IT'S GOOD TO BE KING

**"And one day when the journey ends
And you see yourself through an unforgiven lens
Still, I'm gonna shout, I'm gonna sing
That sometimes, it's good to be king"**

(2008)

Dying wasn't something Dave had ever really planned for. Literally. He had no rolodex. No scheduler. No agenda and most notably, no life insurance policy or even a will. But now as he lay in the guest bedroom of his oldest son's house, he let out a heavy sigh, wondering if this approach had been a mistake.

It's just another birthday, he thought to himself, turning to look over at Sandy who was still fast asleep at his side. But in his gut, he knew his sixtieth would be his last.

Dave looked up at the ceiling. Ribbons of colorful light danced above him thanks to a suncatcher Sandy had put in the windowsill. It was a nice room, with clean white walls and a sunny disposition. The house was built a little too well for Dave's taste. But he was proud of his son for being able to afford it, and given the circumstances, happy to reap whatever benefits he could.

Over the last few weeks, the room had become somewhat a of a home away from home for Dave whenever he needed to be closer to the hospital. But that wasn't the occasion today. The doctors down at Mass General were giving him a month off from the aggressive chemo treatments that were sapping his vitality. And his children were planning a big party for him tonight.

Dave had been rather ambivalent about the idea of a party. For the first time in his life, he was feeling self-conscious, and it was hard to fathom any of his old friends or lovers seeing him now like this. He could do without the pity. Secretly, He had hoped that maybe if he just didn't mention it, his kids would forget the whole idea of a party, and it would all go away. But this approach had failed. And now here he was, wondering when life just started happening to him like this.

Sitting up in bed, Dave spotted a familiar photograph hanging on the wall, across the room He was seated on his favorite motorcycle, with Lennie comfortably in his lap. "Fuck!" Dave muttered to himself looking jealously at his younger and vibrant self.

Maybe I can beat this, he thought to himself.

It wasn't an unreasonable possibility. After all he was a guy that had lived decades in the company of more than his share of beautiful women, had accumulated enough wealth to last several lifetimes, and never – until now – had suffered from as much as a bad cold.

Besides, he was still a father to his three kids and a grandfather to a couple grandchildren. And even with the heavy lifting of parenthood behind him, he knew that he hadn't yet passed onto his family everything that life had taught him. He just needed to stretch things out a little longer.

With little left to do but start the day, Dave lifted the sheets and peered down at the stump where his leg used to be. Who was he kidding. He was dying. That much was clear.

———————————

Dave looked over at Sandy who was still lost in slumber. He had no idea how anyone could stay asleep in bed once sunlight filled a room. With a little effort he turned away from her and moved to the edge of the bed, to put on his bathrobe and … one sock.

He reached down and picked up the floppy white thing. He was still getting used to the feeling of only dressing one foot but took some comfort in knowing he would never again have to worry about losing a sock from a pair. He wondered if it would be possible for him to purchase only one shoe at a discounted rate next time that he needed one.

With his robe secured and his sock in place, Dave reached over and picked up a book from one of the small crates next to his bed. It was his old journal, something he had dug up recently after life had started taking hold of him in this new and uncomfortable way.

For the first decade of his life in Maine, he had written in the journal on a consistent basis, imaging some importance and uniqueness to his experience. Flipping through the pages Dave realized what a fool he had been. Young, strong and hopeful for the future. But, at some point ten years in, he had simply stopped documenting the distance that separated him from where he had started.

Settling back into what was now a well-worn groove in his mattress, he opened to the inside cover of the journal and read the first words he had written to himself upon his arrival in western Maine.

JOURNAL ENTRY
May 12th, 1971

To my future self—

Well, it's official. Today Rachel and I signed the papers on the new land and said goodbye and good riddance to the way life was and honestly, I'm feeling optimistic about this whole new adventure. Rachel seems excited too. It took some convincing…Not everybody's made for the rural life you know, but she'll figure it out, I'm sure.

We've been married for almost 5 months now and after kind of a shaky start it finally feels like we're finding our way. Having a few kids will be our next step, and I know she's eager for that. But first we need to make a home and even though we've only been in Maine for less than a week, this place seems just perfect!

For years back in Boston, I used to read the real estate ads in the Sunday Globe for cheap land in Western Maine. I wonder if they had guys like me in mind when they ran those ads. Well, it's too late now and this wandering Jew isn't leaving anytime soon.

The wife is not a fan of the ride into our land. Mud has taken over the road that leads up to where we plan on building our house. I told her not to worry and that this was probably just an aberration. But she's probably going to have to trade in her office heels for some tall muck boots, because I'm almost certain that I'm not telling her the truth.

Last week was my final week teaching at Newton South elementary back in the city. And…my last paycheck for a while. But I'm not that worried. I would never say this to Rachel after working so hard convincing her to leave behind her family, her friends, a secure job, and the life she knew…but a part of me will miss my 5th grade class. I think what I liked most about it was that I could walk to school from our little place in the city. That's not going to be an option for me here! (Who am I kidding? What I liked most was servicing the lonely mom's)

But most of me is glad to be out of that place. No more school drama. No late nights lying in bed worrying about stupid shit like getting yelled at by the principal for taking my class on unauthorized field trips, bringing animals into the classroom, the way I dressed, or my general lack of cleanliness. To be honest the only reason I decided to take that teaching job in the first place was to avoid getting drafted.

Maine feels like the place where it's ok to break the rules a little. There's really no one around to judge. Hell, I can't even see the neighbor's house from our land. Anyway, I feel ready. Or I feel mostly ready, for the tradeoff. And this place, being closer to nature, staying in the moment, it all just feels right. Like I've got a purpose here. Something meaningful.

Dave stopped, closed the journal and let out a sigh. He placed it back on the nightstand and turned back to his sleeping girlfriend.

"Sandy…" he said, giving her a gentle shake. "…wake up!" He needed the company of another human.

"Not now," she moaned plaintively, moving a pillow over her eyes.

But Dave persisted. "No, I swear I'm not looking to get any right now. I just want to talk."

Sandy was skeptical, and she wasn't ready to give up the blissful feeling of being halfway between worlds. But as she remembered his birthday, possibly his last at that, she lifted the pillow from her face and began rubbing her blurry eyes. "What do you need Dave?"

Dave stared at her patiently, and as her eyes came into focus, she could tell that this was indeed not a call for morning sex. His face wore a serious look. "Is everything all right?" she asked him.

"What kind of guys do you think you'll be with after I'm gone?" He was feeling curious about what her plans were once he was out of the picture.

"What?" Sandy was unsure of how to respond. "I don't know, I… I just woke up Dave."

But his face didn't change, and he waited for an answer.

She gave a little laugh. "You really want me to tell you who I might want to be with after you're gone. Right now? right here? On the morning of your birthday? Sweetie, I'm not really feeling like having a relationship is going to be a priority for me anytime soon," she answered honestly. "Seven years we've been together and, like your son always says, its dog years, so that makes for nearly five decades of your shit! You think I want more?"

Dave nodded. She was laughing now, and for a moment they both felt almost normal.

Sandy took a deep breath and the drew in closer to Dave, before whispering in his ear. "Lay back!"

Obediently, Dave did as he was told. Sandy began nibbling

on his ear, kissing his neck, and then began rubbing his chest rhythmically. As her hands gradually worked their way down to his hardening cock, Sandy kept her eyes on Dave's face and watched as some semblance of life was restored in his system. Once she had finished, she returned her head to her pillow and fell back asleep.

———

A half hour later Sandy returned to consciousness, finding Dave awake and thumbing through a book she didn't recognize. After a brief yawn, she asked him, "What are you looking at?"

"It's an old journal of mine from the 1970's," Dave replied before returning the book to the crate. He wasn't sure about sharing the burden with her at this moment. "When I used to be optimistic," he continued, gently wrapping Sandy up in his tired arms.

Outside the room, there was a loud knock. "Dad? Are you up?" Lennie's voice asked from the other side of the door.

"We'll be down soon!" Dave replied. It was time to pull it together for his family and just make the best of the day.

This was probably how it was going to end. Surrounded by his kids – and nothing else really mattered.

———

"Hey Dad…how are you feeling on your big day?" asked his oldest son optimistically as Sandy walked his father over to a chair in the kitchen.

"I'm not dead yet! Right sweetie?" Dave turned and gave a little wink at his girlfriend before joining his oldest son at the kitchen table.

"I'm going to go and take a shower," she said shaking her head.

"Okay, but don't be gone too long or I might not make it!" her boyfriend replied jokingly.

"Not funny!" Sandy shouted, lifting a raised eyebrow and walking off.

"Now, who's making me breakfast today?" Dave had joyfully discovered how willing others were to cook and prepare meals for a dying man, something he had always struggled to do on his own.

"I've got you covered!" said Lennie's wife Danielle as she cheerfully approached the table. Still in her own cheetah print robe and fluffy white slippers, she placed a plate of sliced oranges in front of him.

The kid had done well for himself, thought Dave, appreciating the scene in front of him. Nice house. Check. Hot wife. Check.

"The usual?" she inquired, and her father in-law nodded. As his daughter-in-law walked away, he took a moment to appreciate her well constructed backside.

It was not unnoticed by his son. "Really Dad?" That's my wife."

"First off Lennie, don't worry, I'm only admiring the view. And second… where's a pen?" Dave looked from side to side. "You should really be writing this stuff down. I've only got so much time left to share these life lessons with you."

"My memory is still pretty good dad – I don't think I'll need a pen," his son replied sarcastically as he reached over the table for an orange slice.

"Who taught you to be such a smug little – whatever," and Dave waved his hand. "The point is, you never stop appreciating a woman's body, no matter how old you get."

Lennie just shook his head and grinned. "So…" he spoke slowly and deliberately now, "…tell me Dad, what's your plan?"

"What do you mean?" his father asked, sensing that this was just going to be a continuation of their on-going discussion about his will. Or lack thereof.

Dave had been avoiding the issue for at least six months in the face of his son's persistent reminders, and he had yet to commit anything in writing. In return, his son felt obligated to remind his father daily that his lack of action, was not going to make it easy for the rest of them after he was gone.

"You know what I mean," Lennie said exasperated. He didn't

feel like it was too much to ask his dad for this small consideration, given just how complicated Dave's finances and real estate holdings were likely to be.

"Stop worrying," offered his dad reassuringly. "I am making too much money to die!"

It was true that he had indeed found some unique revenue sources thanks to his illness, including re-selling the Oxycontin pills he was hording. His cancer diagnosis had given him access to a wide variety of painkillers, and he was unloading them as quickly as he qualified for re-fills.

"Dad, I'm serious. For just a minute can you think about the rest of us and what we're going to be left with after all this shit is over with?" he regretted the words as soon as they escaped his mouth.

"I'm just going to leave it all to you!" Dave blurt out, quickly deciding that he actually meant it. "You figure it out!" He felt the tears building in his eyes and his son realized just how badly it was hurting his to father to consider this kind of discussion.

"OK, Dad," Lennie said quietly. "I'll take care of it."

After breakfast, Dave retrieved the create of books from the guestroom and made his way over to the EZ chair in his son's family room. From there he had a great view out the window, allowing him a glimpse of Danielle as she prepared for her morning dip. But once she was submerged, there was little remaining in the way of distraction, and he began to methodically sift through his book's one by one.

Each of the books had mapped a piece of his journey through the 1970's. There were the writings of Thoreau and Emerson; both of whom had helped inspire Dave and his first wife to leave Boston for western Maine. There were also books from homesteaders like Scott and Helen Nearing whose ideas had contributed guidance to the couple's first few years in the state, with writing that was always a bit more practical than the Massachusetts transcendentalists.

Ironically, after becoming a father, Dave's tastes had once again pivoted, this time to the novels of Louis L'Amour – whose mythical frontier allowed a man to be a man, minus any of the confusing contemporary baggage. He now realized that it was likely that some of his tastes had changed simply because he had an easier time imagining himself getting laid in L'Amour's world than in Thoreau's.

And as far as the asceticism of the Nearing's went, that had never really been a good fit for him. There was something too austere about their ideals, too detached from the pleasures of life. He liked a good steak, a comfortable chair, and a cold beer as much as the next guy, and the notion of retreating to a back-to-the-land existence, surviving on vegetables and a strict regimen, had faded over time.

Opening his old journal, he again began re-reading some of the entries from what now felt like a strange and distant life.

JOURNAL ENTRY
November 20th, 1971

Is it me, or is the snow fall here in Maine just somehow better than it was back home? More magical or maybe just cleaner than snow in the city. Back in Massachusetts we usually wouldn't even see the first signs of snow until after Thanksgiving.

Up in these hills it's like we're dealing with a whole other creature, and I've got my fingers crossed that we're ready for it. The woodstove does a decent job keeping the cabin warm enough for my standards, but not Rachels. We've picked up some heavy quilts, but I'm going to probably need to make love to her on a regular basis to keep it bearable! What are you going to do?

Thankfully we got the roof on the house right before Halloween, so that's good! Speaking of Halloween, we've still got a whole bag of candy at the house. Rachel didn't know whether to expect for trick or treaters around here. It's not like the suburbs I told her, but she didn't listen. Women never do.

I feel like a godman author or something sitting here by the woodstove writing in my journal.

"You alright?" Lennie checked in as he pulled up a seat next to his father.

Dave put down the journal and offered up a new thought. "You know… you know there's that picture in my room… I mean your guestroom…"

"Yeah, the one where I'm sitting on your lap?"

"Yeah, that's the one." Dave gave a wistful sigh. "You were so little back then, and I was always so busy planning this, scheming that… sometimes I feel like I missed, I mean… well I… I like to believe I was a good Dad to you… and your siblings." He felt an overwhelming sadness rolling up inside of him. and swallowed hard in his best attempt to hold back tears.

"You were a good Dad. No one would ever question that," his son reassured him. "Except maybe the authorities."

For a few minutes they sat in silence. Finally, Lennie asked, "You ready for the party?"

Dave lied. "Sure!"

CHAPTER 23

IT'S NOT EASY IN THE SHADOW OF A GOD

**"But who's got time like that to waste
A wise man asked me to my face
If they wrote a book about your life
Would anyone care besides your wife"**

(2008)

Dave headed out to the back yard set-up and surveyed what his children had put in motion. "*They're not as cheap as I am!*" he thought, looking around at the scene—there were tubs full of beer and ice, a high-tech grill, and picnic tables ready for an onslaught of side dishes and condiments that Sandy was helping Danielle prepare in the kitchen at this very moment.

Dave's own backyard parties at the sauna were mostly a blur now, but one thing he was sure of: they'd never looked like this. The most his hazy memory could conjure was a few beat-up coolers, cheap beer, hamburgers, red hotdogs, and maybe some potato salad. But that was only if someone's girlfriend had thought to bring it.

But this… this was next level. And he had to admit, Lennie had probably learned how to throw a real party from his mother, because it sure as hell wasn't from him.

Just then the sliding door open and Sandy came out with two glasses of ice-cold lemonade.

"Can I offer you a drink?" she asked light heartedly.

Sandy placed the glasses on a small table beside Dave and then pulled a prescription pill bottle from her pocket. "I brought your pills!" she said and positioned the container by the drinks, before pulling up a seat next to her boyfriend in the warm afternoon sunlight.

"Thank you, sweetie!" Dave reached for the pills and a glass.

"Of course," she replied.

It was liberating knowing that he wasn't going to live long enough to worry about any side effects from the pill popping. He dropped an Oxy into his mouth and washed it down with some lemonade.

"Just think," he said. "When I'm gone, you'll be able to live like this all the time."

Sandy looked at him confused.

"Oh, you know what I mean... no more unbearable weekly trips with me down to the hospital in Boston where you get to witness my transformation into a living jack ass."

—————

It was true that the trips south had become almost unbearable, with Dave's moods ranging from cranky to open hostility at the hospital staff. The obvious futility of the treatments had become apparent to everyone and maintaining the façade was overwhelming for everyone involved.

Dave was not built for hospitals, and it had all come to a head during a recent chemo session when became convinced that the intern responsible for setting up the port into his vein had missed the mark, and that the chemo was now leaking into the surrounding tissues. It was an unsettling possibility, and he grew agitated trying to convince the staff that he wasn't delusional.

"I want it x-rayed!" Dave said, quietly chastising himself for allowing a novice anywhere near his body. "Nothing's going in until that happens!" he insisted as a swell of anger and genuine fear came to the surface. He had no intention of continuing with what was probably a futile treatment until they took a closer look.

Faced with Dave's ultimatum, the hospital had him wheeled to the X-ray technician's office, where his suspicions were quickly confirmed. The port indeed had a crack, and just as Dave had feared, chemo was now spilling into places where it was not supposed to go.

Fuck! he thought to himself. Dying of cancer was one thing. Dying because some dumb shit kid who didn't even have a medical license had fucked up a simple procedure, would be another.

"You guys are lucky I'm almost dead!" Dave said only half-jokingly to the doctor on his return to the room. "Otherwise, I'd sue you!" But even if he did have a legal leg to stand on, he'd be gone long before a lawsuit would reach the courts. And truthfully, lawyers still made him nervous.

————

"Well…no more trips to the hospital would be nice, but I don't know about the rest. I mean your kids are great and everything. But without you here with me, I'm an outsider. We all know that. I don't think we'll be spending all that much time together in your absence." Sandy lamented.

Dave studied her for a moment. She was right. His kids were good to her, but she wasn't really family. The kids already had moms and having her around after their father was gone would only reinforce this.

"Well at the very least then, if you want to stay connected to the family, I give you permission to sleep with any of my sons or even daughter I suppose. But the rule is, I gotta be dead first!"

"Really Dave? Don't worry, I'm all good." She shook her head and shot him a look.

Dave withdrew a tiny vile of coke from the pocket of his cut-off blue jean shorts. If he was going to make it through this party, he was going to need all the help he could get.

"Little early for that wouldn't you say?" teased Sandy.

"Don't worry, I can share, but I have to say it's going to cost you…" he teased her back and began unzipping his pants. Sandy shook her head. Tenderness tinged with depravity. Depravity tinged with tenderness. Dave's favorite love language.

"You get nothing until after the birthday cake is cut!". And with that Sandy headed back inside to see what was left to do in the kitchen.

"Jeesus, get some candles on that thing. I'm on a tight schedule!" he joked as she walked off.

———

By the time Dave woke up after a late afternoon nap and returned outside, the yard was full of friends and family. Scanning the crowd, he spotted his old buddy Veiko and his wife Maria standing together over on the grass, and he remembered his role getting them together a decade earlier.

His sightline was interrupted by Saul's arrival. "Hey, Boss Man. Still falling a little short in all the same places?"

"Yeah, that's the fate of every Jewish guy. You know that as well as I do!" he retorted and for a few minutes they settled into their usual routine of busting each other's balls.

"Happy fucking birthday to me!" Dave said with a bitter chuckle, accepting a fat joint his buddy offered. "Last time around the sun!"

"Death and fucking taxes, buddy," Saul said. "They come for all of us!"

Leaning into the dark humor, Dave offered his own take. "Well at least I'll be able to say that I dodged taxes better than you."

———

"David!" came an all too familiar voice from behind the birthday boy.

"Nancy!" he said turning to see his ex-wife approaching. By now, time and circumstances had dissipated the post-divorce baggage they each carried. She wrapped her arms around his frail body, and whispered gently into his ear, "How are you doing, sweetie?"

"I've been better," Dave answered honestly. "But it's not so bad, there are a lot of perks to being sick you know!"

"I can only imagine…" she said with a laugh. "Hey… look at the kids," she smiled nodding in the direction of their children. All three of them were standing near the firepit and laughing at one of Dave's grandchildren, who was valiantly trying to walk.

"You did that you know," he said to Nancy.

"Did what?" she asked a little puzzled.

"Raised them right!" Dave replied. "Hell, Lennie isn't even yours, but you loved him like he had been birthed from your own womb."

Nancy blushed "So, now you're going to start appreciating me?" But there was no trace of animosity in her voice.

"I've always appreciated you, Nancy. I've just never been any good at showing it. I remember from the beginning…" he continued "…you always had three children, never two children and a stepchild. It made a difference you know. You made us a family. I don't think I could have done the same for someone else's child."

Nancy was taken aback, and she stayed silent as she clasped her hands over his.

"Remember what I used to tell the kids when they were growing up? About the very basics of life?", he whispered to her. "*Halt aakh nisht groys. Farsheymt kaynem nisht. Ir zent nisht beser fin kaynem aynem. In verts nisht fet*"

"I remember David. It means…" she paused to take a breath, "…stay humble. Never show someone up. You are not better than anybody. And don't get fat." She looked him over. "Seems like you've managed to heed some of your own advice?"

"I'd like to think I'm trying," Dave said with a sigh.

____

"I'll tell you the real reason that people came to the sauna. It's because I never let assholes hang out there. People who imagine themselves on a higher plain then the rest of us. They're everywhere. Even in western Maine." By now, Dave was drunk and thoroughly enjoying the spotlight given over to a dying man. "I mean, I wasn't perfect, but I wasn't hiding from the world and judging it from a distance like those assholes."

"Yeah, you judged it perfectly well from your chair!" Nancy chimed in, excited at the opportunity to set the record straight for the assembled crowd, which had been growing larger as her ex-husbands voice had increased in volume and intensity

"I probably should have stayed back in Massachusetts. But…" he paused, "… they didn't want me either!" he laughed. "Same with the folks living up on the hill. I mean, some of them got their weed from me…maybe a few other things," he added with a mischievous smile. "But they never actually invited me into their homes…and god forbid one of their daughters or wives spent any time down at the sauna," he was rambling now. "I know I didn't personally scare them. But the idea of me sure did"

"David, you sound just like that guy in Easy Rider!" Nancy laughed.

He was busted. Long ago, like every other hippie, he had memorized the movies famous monologue. It had only taken him almost forty years to find the right time to use it.

———

By 11:30PM most of the beer on-site had been consumed and the firepit was down to mostly embers. Folks were beginning to trickle away and even Sandy had departed back to Oxford Hills where she hoped to get some much-needed rest and to also let the dog out before it pissed all over the house again.

By the time Saul was ready to make his departure Dave had already landed on his best material for the awkward departures of friends and family. "Thanks for coming tonight, Saul…hey, umm…

things are a little tight. Do you think I could borrow some cash before you go? I can repay you in a few months." It was the third time he had used the line, and it was still getting laughs.

Saul knelt in front of Dave's chair, gently pulled his friend closer to him, and gave him an extended hug. "I love you!" he whispered to his friend. After a minute, the two men disengaged from their embrace. Saul turned and headed towards his vehicle, holding back the tears just long enough to get out of the view.

———

Dave felt the nip of the 1am air as he hobbled across the yard and towards the warmth of his son's outdoor hot tub. He passed dozens of empty beer cans and paper plates scattered on the lawn and even a random pair of panties strung up on one of the tree branches. By the looks of the aftermath, it appeared that his last hurrah had been a good one.

Much to his pleasure, Dave found that the hot tub was currently occupied by two of his oldest son's female friends, both comfortably naked inside the soothing waters.

"Mind if I join you?" he asked.

"Hop on in birthday boy!" the women closer to him said, giving him a playful splash.

Between the drugs in his system and his crutches, it took Dave a moment to make his way into the water. He fished out a half empty vile of cocaine from earlier in the afternoon, set it on the side of the tub, and climbed in. The water felt almost perfect set against the cool night air.

Dave glanced briefly up at the stars, before turning his attention back to the other hot tub occupants.

"You girls like to party?" he inquired.

"Would we be sitting in a hot tub at one in the morning if we didn't?" one of them wise cracked.

A few minutes and a couple lines later, Dave felt almost like a rock star. He took a moment to look over his own naked body, now soaking in the water. His leg had been the first part of him to go and up until this point it had caused him nothing but a sense of embarrassment and inconvenience.

But now, the cocaine confidence swimming in his brain offered him with a new line of thinking. A smile grew across his face as he thought to himself, *look how much bigger my dick looks next to the stump!*

CHAPTER 24

WHEN I DIE, BURY ME IN MY CUT OFF BLUE JEANS

"When I die bury me in my cut-off blue jeans
When I go send all my money with me
When I leave don't come looking for me
When I die bury me in my cut-off blue jeans"

(2008)

It was a tranquil morning, with only the sound of birdsongs filtering through the slightly open bedroom window. The world outside still clung to the dampness of early spring, but inside, in the quiet of the bedroom, the first tendrils of light began creeping across the floor.

Dave felt a deep, almost spiritual reluctance to leave his dream state, where the weight of his deteriorating body didn't press so heavily on him. Floating at the edge of consciousness for as long as possible seemed like the smart move.

Unfortunately, the early morning anxiety of their young dog made staying asleep impossible, and as his eyes opened, the gentle pull of reality began to tighten its grip. Thankfully, the room was bathed in soft sunlight, and for a few more minutes he was able to lay still, listening to the rhythmic sound of Sandy's breathing beside him.

Through the large glass window in his bedroom the White Mountains stretched out in the distance, now partially obscured by a thick fog. Beside him, his girlfriend's form seemed to blend into the chaos of the sheets. Lying next to her was the half-naked body of the woman they'd met only the night before.

A small cluster of prescription bottles sat on the nightstand. OxyContin, Percocet, Oxycodone—pills Dave had come to rely on to ease the pain of his failing health. After selecting his morning regimen, he reached for the water bottle that rested beside the small containers, his fingers shaking slightly. He emptied out a few pills, swallowed the medication, and turned back to Sandy who had begun to stir.

"Here's to the pharmaceutical industry!" he declared, raising his glass before taking a large gulp of water.

Sandy's eyes fluttered open, her hand instinctively reaching up to rub at the exhaustion in her face. She offered no smile, no playful retort, just a quiet resignation in her gaze. The constant cycle of hospitals, medications, and long stretches with little said between them was bad enough. Waking up with another woman in their bed, again, was pushing her to her limit.

A long, strained silence hung in the room. Dave broke it with a half-smile, his voice laced with humor. "You're not gonna cry, are you? Come on, Sandy!" he said softly, misinterpreting the tightness in her face for sorrow over his illness. "You'll be fine after I go. You'll have the house all to yourself. Take as many lovers as you want. I won't be around to beat them up!"

His girlfriend's eyes darkened and the tension in her face shifted from sadness to something sharper, something harder. "You think I give a shit about that right now?" she snapped, her voice tight with unspent emotion.

Dave froze and the playful tone vanished from his face. He wasn't sure what hurt more: the sharpness of her words or the coldness with which she said them. He watched her roll away from him, with a quiet resolve.

"I need to go take a shower," she muttered, pulling herself out of bed with a practiced fluidity.

"Sandy…" Dave began, his voice was soft, almost pleading as he reached out to her. But she ignored him, slipping out of the sheets with a quiet finality.

He watched her disappear down the hall, purposedly avoiding his gaze and not looking back. After a few moments, he heard the distant sound of the water turning on in the bathroom. After her brief shower, she quietly left for the day, taking the collie with her, and uncertain about when she would be back.

———

A few hours later, Dave finally dragged his aching body out of bed. He shuffled to the bathroom, reluctantly looking into the mirror as he passed. Over the last few months, his beard had grown scruffy, his face pale and increasingly hollow, and he was thankful that it was the only mirror in the house.

After a challenging shower, he returned to the bedroom to find that their overnight guest had also departed, leaving behind only disheveled sheets. He dressed in the first clothes he could find—flannel shirt, faded jeans, and a pair of weathered boots and relocated to the kitchen where he stared out the window.

Everything about the house has been designed with simplicity in mind, a quiet monument to Dave's minimalist aesthetic. The walls were still unfinished in places, the structure more an open suggestion of a home than a conventional dwelling. There were no curtains on the windows, just heavy drapes that barely hinted at the concept of privacy. And the bathroom, as Sandy often reminded him, was the kind that only a man could love.

Before he had become sick, the house had represented a new start for Sandy and himself. But after the illness set in, the home had begun feeling cold and uninviting. The lack of history meant nothing for Dave to hold onto. No marks on the wall with his kids' heights. No stain on the carpet where one of the kids' dogs had puked. And certainly, no photos of his ex-wife, who he had spent over two decades with.

With a low groan, he hobbled out of the house, his stiff limbs protesting every movement. His car seemed like the best option for something familiar, and he slowly made his way over to the vehicle. He climbed into the driver's seat and gripped the wheel like it was an anchor, before reaching over and turning the radio on. But it was too much, and he quickly turned it off in favor of just the dull hum of the engine.

As he rested there, he thought back to his first few years in Maine when he and his first wife, would drive aimlessly with absolutely no intention in mind. The past seemed so distant and surreal now and he envied the folks nearing the end of life lucky enough to have already lost their memories.

Reaching over to the glove compartment he pulled out a small stash of homegrown cannabis. After carefully filling his pipe, his hands searched for a lighter behind the car's paperwork and repair receipts. Finding nothing, he reached down under the front of his seat, rummaged through the accumulated trash, and located a Bic that still held fluid.

With a practiced motion, he lit the pipe and took a long drag. Letting the smoke fill his lungs, he braced himself for the painful cough that usually followed. He was grateful when the moment passed, and he had been spared. The calming rush settling into his brain was just what his weary body needed.

Dave reclined back in his seat, feeling the worn fabric beneath him. He exhaled slowly, the smoke curling out of the cracked window. He glanced at the dash, and let his finger trace the edges of the worn leather steering wheel.

The world outside was getting ready to move on without him. Dave closed his eyes and took a deep breath.

He had to admit, *it had been a hell of a run.*

EPILOGUE

(2012)

"Dad, I think I found something!" Dave's grandson, Ethan, burst into the sauna lounge, breathless. His voice cracked with excitement as he skidded to a stop near the pool table where his father, Walter, was playing a game with a few regulars.

Walter hopped off his stool. "Found what?"

The young boy's wide eyes were nearly popping out of his head. "Out back, by the woodshed! You gotta come, quick! I—I don't know what it is, but it's a lot of stuff!"

"Guess I'll be back in a second." He leaned the pool stick against the wall and headed down back through the door and into the woodshed where three of Ethan's friends were gathered around a cinder block. The block had been dislodged from the wall, likely from some roughhousing, and now it revealed a hidden space beneath. The kids were peering inside with wide-eyed fascination, as if they'd stumbled upon a secret entrance.

"Let me take a look!" Walter asked in a calm voice. He peered into the exposed chamber, its dark interior filled with a haphazard collection of old coffee cans, some rusted, some still in decent shape.

One of the boys, a freckled kid named Timmy, looked up at him nervously. "We didn't mean to, Mr. Gravier! We were just playing, and the block—well, it moved, and we saw this stuff in there."

Walter crouched down and peered inside. He could barely make out the shape of dozens of coffee cans in the hole and he carefully reached into the darkness and pulled one out. He could feel the weight of something inside and he carefully set the can on top of a nearby barrel, before pealing back the lid. His eyes widened in disbelief. Inside was what appeared to be a lump of hardened paraffin wax, surrounded by a large roll of bills. He knocked the can on the barrel a few times and the loosened contents dropped out.

"Dad…what is it?" Ethan asked, watching his father with wide, anxious eyes.

Walter didn't answer immediately. He picked up another can, then another, pulling them one by one from the chamber. It took only a few moments, but soon he had a small pile of cans stacked up on the barrel. His hands were shaking slightly, and by the time he was done emptying the cans there were dozens of blocks of paraffin staring back at him.

Walter turned to the other boys, who were still staring at the cans with wide eyes. "You all stay right here. Don't touch anything. Not even a finger." He met each of their gazes and held it long enough to make sure they understood.

He turned on his heel and quickly made his way back toward the sauna. The sound of his boots hitting the wooden deck echoed in the quiet night. His mind was racing. The bills inside those cans—there was no mistaking it. This was the money. The money his father, Dave, had lost years ago. Walter's heart pounded in his chest as he strode inside, heading straight for his cell phone on the bar.

Dialing Lennie's number, Walter's hand trembled as he brought the phone to his ear. It rang twice before his older brother answered.

"Hey, what's going on?" Lennie's voice came through the line.

"You need to get over here. We found it!" his younger brother blurted out.

"Found what?" Lennie's asked. But as soon as he said the words, he knew exactly what Walter was talking about. "No way. Are you serious?"

"Yeah, I'm serious. It's all in the woodshed, covered in paraffin and hidden in old coffee cans. I'm waiting for you guys before I go any further," his brother assured him.

"I'm on my way. Call Heidi. Tell her to get over here too. This is big."

"Already on it," Walter responded, but Lennie had already hung up.

Walter quickly punched in his sister's number.

"Wait, what?" Heidi asked, incredulous. "Are you serious?"

"I'm dead serious," Walter replied. "Get over here, now!"

————

An hour later, the three of them—Walter, Lennie, and Heidi—were sitting at the bar in the sauna, their eyes fixed on the piles of cash now spread out on the counter in front of them. Rolls of hundred-dollar bills filled the space, each bundle carefully wrapped with faded rubber bands.

The siblings fell silent as they began to count the bills, their fingers expertly peeling each one off and laying it flat on the pool table. As they worked, they took turns poking fun at their dad.

"Remember how he thought Mom had gotten it while he was down in the Bahama's?" Heidi laughed.

"I was kind of proud of her!" said Walter. "He owes her an apology. And maybe a nice dinner."

Lennie grinned. "Too little, too late."

Heidi smiled, and as if reading from a defense lawyers handbook she said, "That god it's just under the $10,000 amount that requires us to report it to the IRS…right?"

Lennie raised a glass in mock salute. "Dad certainly taught us well."

Photo Credits: Nancy Graiver